"Beverly, i... fleet rules ...
lation program."

As if that would stop someone from actually doing it, Beverly thought. "Unless you had the correct authorization," she replied out loud.

"That is true." Data leaned closer. "Are you contemplating doing something illegal with a holodeck simulation?"

"No, Data, not at all. One of my friends is in trouble because of this 'accident.' And I really want to help, but I can't seem to figure out what happened."

"I assume your friend does not have the expertise to change a simulation." Beverly nodded. The android continued. "No doubt Commander Wiley was in the holodeck at the time. He is known as one of the best simulations experts in Starfleet. He would have the authorization to change a simulation."

"Why create a shock that might injure a cadet?"

"Perhaps you should ask the Commander."

Beverly stood up. "Thank you. You're absolutely right. It's time to confront Commander Wiley again. And this time I want the Admiral there."

Star Trek: The Next Generation
STARFLEET ACADEMY

Star Trek: Deep Space Nine

Star Trek movie tie-in

Star Trek Generations

Available from MINSTREL Books

STAR TREK
THE NEXT GENERATION®

STARFLEET ACADEMY® #10

LOYALTIES

Patricia Barnes-Svarney

Interior illustrations by
Todd Cameron Hamilton

A MINSTREL®
BOOK

Published by POCKET BOOKS
New York   London   Toronto   Sydney   Tokyo   Singapore

A MINSTREL PAPERBACK *Original*

A Minstrel Book published by
POCKET BOOKS, a division of Simon & Schuster Inc.
1230 Avenue of the Americas, New York, NY 10020

STAR TREK is a Registered Trademark of
A VIACOM COMPANY Paramount Pictures.

This book is published by Pocket Books, a division of Simon & Schuster Inc., under exclusive license from Paramount Pictures.

ISBN: 0-671-55280-5

First Minstrel Books printing April 1996

10 9 8 7 6 5 4 3 2 1

A MINSTREL BOOK and colophon are registered trademarks of Simon & Schuster Inc.

Cover art by Donato Giancola

Printed in the U.S.A.

To Helen, Billy, and the Bear

STARFLEET TIMELINE

2264

The launch of Captain James T. Kirk's five-year mission, _U.S.S. Enterprise,_ NCC-1701.

2292

Alliance between the Klingon Empire and the Romulan Star Empire collapses.

2293

Colonel Worf, grandfather of Worf Rozhenko, defends Captain Kirk and Doctor McCoy at their trial for the murder of Klingon chancellor Gorkon.

Khitomer Peace Conference, Klingon Empire/Federation (_Star Trek VI_).

2323

Jean-Luc Picard enters Starfleet Academy's standard four-year program.

2328

The Cardassian Empire annexes the Bajoran homeworld.

2341

Data enters Starfleet Academy.

2342

Beverly Crusher (née Howard) enters Starfleet Academy Medical School, an eight-year program.

2346

Romulan massacre of Klingon outpost on Khitomer.

2351

In orbit around Bajor, the Cardassians construct a space station that they will later abandon.

2353

William T. Riker and Geordi La Forge enter Starfleet Academy.

2354

Deanna Troi enters Starfleet Academy.

2356

Tasha Yar enters Starfleet Academy.

2357

Worf Rozhenko enters Starfleet Academy.

2363

Captain Jean-Luc Picard assumes command of U.S.S. Enterprise, NCC-1701-D.

2367

Wesley Crusher enters Starfleet Academy.

An uneasy truce is signed between the Cardassians and the Federation.

Borg attack at Wolf 359; First Officer Lieutenant Commander Benjamin Sisko and his son, Jake, are among the survivors.

U.S.S. Enterprise-D defeats the Borg vessel in orbit around Earth.

2369

Commander Benjamin Sisko assumes command of Deep Space Nine in orbit over Bajor.

Source: Star Trek® Chronology / Michael Okuda and Denise Okuda

CHAPTER

1

Beverly Howard was *not* in a good mood.

She grit her teeth as she remembered her morning. First, she couldn't find her comm badge. Then she had to crawl between her bed and desk to retrieve a dropped data chip for her morning History of Disease class. On her test, she couldn't recall the year the plasma plague broke out on the planet Obi VI. On top of that, the professor assigned more homework than anyone expected and held the class over by five minutes.

And now she was trying to quickly eat her lunch in the cafeteria before her next class—while staring wide-eyed at her roommate, Claire Voy.

"You want to *what?*" Beverly managed to ask between bites of food.

"I said let's skip class," said Claire.

Beverly shook her head in disbelief. She met Claire

on the transport vessel traveling to Starfleet Academy, neither cadet knowing they were assigned to the same room. She discovered they had plenty in common: Both were born on Luna colony, on the Earth's moon. Both lived on several different planets while they were growing up. And both wanted to become doctors.

But they differed greatly in physical appearance. Beverly was medium height and slender. She had long, straight red hair and fair skin. Claire was a few inches shorter than Beverly and slightly stocky. Her complexion was olive, with straight, short black hair that matched her dark eyes.

Beverly stopped eating and stared at her roommate. "Skip class?"

"Skip class," Claire echoed, nodding. "But it's for a good cause."

"Good cause?"

"Bev, you're repeating everything I say," she said, tilting her head in frustration. "Remember the Old San Francisco archaeological dig, on the edge of the Academy campus?" Beverly nodded. For about a year, archaeologists had been uncovering several buildings damaged from a major earthquake two centuries ago. Yesterday's big news around campus was the cave-in at the dig—part of the area had collapsed the night before. "I talked to an upperclassman who's helping with the dig. They're opening part of the exposed section of the cave-in today—and it's a twenty-first century hospital!"

"Hospital?"

"Bev, you're doing it again."

They stopped talking as a cadet neared their table. Beverly waited until he walked by. "Claire, we just can't skip class," she continued, whispering desperately to her roommate, "especially Terran Anatomy. We're reviewing for the next test, remember?"

Claire pushed back a lock of her short, dark hair that strayed to her forehead. She leaned closer to Beverly. "Yes, I know. But, Bev, you and I know the human skeleton. We both have the top marks in the class ... well, besides Dewley Breech, of course. This is for our education," Claire pleaded, "and, Bev, it's a hospital, not just some old, moldy stone house."

"I think old, moldy stone houses are pretty interesting," she retorted, smirking at her roommate. "I grew up in one."

"You know what I mean."

Beverly began to eat her lunch again. "You're crazy, Claire. Why don't you just ask me to steal a shuttle and fly to Alpha Centauri instead?"

Claire took a bite of pasta from her plate, then pointed her fork at Beverly. "That's tomorrow. Really, Bev, it won't tarnish your reputation at Starfleet to skip one class. I'm sure even the great cadets of Starfleet probably skipped a class now and then."

Beverly sniffed. "I doubt James T. Kirk would have done such a thing."

"Want to bet?" Claire retorted. "Just what are you really afraid of, Bev? That your grandmother will find out?"

Beverly knew Claire was right. She *was* afraid her grandmother would find out she skipped class—but she was more afraid that she would let her grandmother down.

She had left the comfort of her grandmother's home

on Caldos IV just over three weeks ago. Her grandmother had been her constant companion after her parents died. They had lived in several Federation colonies, her grandmother tending to the sick as a healer and doctor. Beverly learned all about herbs, healing, and medicine from her grandmother.

Because they lived near the wilder, forested areas of the colonies—so her grandmother could collect the healing herbs for her treatments—Beverly was occasionally taught by others in the small, surrounding communities. A tall Vulcan woman who worked on computers at one colony taught Beverly mathematics; on another planet, she learned three languages from the ambassador from New Britain. But her grandmother taught her the most—from Earth history to all the sciences. She also taught her about life and keeping others alive. By watching her grandmother, Beverly knew something by the time she was only twelve years old: She knew she wanted to be a doctor.

Starfleet Academy had not been Beverly's first choice. She originally wanted to attend one of the top medical schools, either the New Johns Hopkins University on Earth, or even Luna colony's Hadley Rill Hospital. But in the end, her grandmother convinced her to try Starfleet Academy. Where else could Beverly learn to be a doctor and still meet so many other species in the galaxy—or experience the adventures she knew Beverly craved? Beverly thought Starfleet Academy would be too hard; her grandmother had faith that Beverly would do well in such a stimulating environment.

But Beverly knew it was not only her grandmother's faith in her that made her feel guilty. There was more.

It was several years since the tragedy at the Federation colony on Arvada III. She and her grandmother lived on the planet during that time, faced tremendous hardship, and survived. They now lived on Caldos IV, and she felt guilty because she had deserted her grandmother to come to the Academy—even though it was her grandmother who encouraged her to enter Starfleet Medical.

"Your grandmother reminds me of Mrs. Oner," said Claire, breaking into Beverly's thoughts. "You know, the woman who owns the small café just off campus. A good cook, caring, a good listener—you should go with me sometime. She makes the best food in this part of the galaxy and uses herbs and spices from all over. She even makes an apple pie from a three-hundred-year-old Earth recipe."

"Maybe she could make a better Gringle Dash," said Beverly, pushing her plate away. "This replicator's version tastes terrible."

"Gringle Dash—that's the dish your grandmother always made you when you felt rotten, right?"

Beverly bit her lip and nodded.

"So—what's your grandmother's name?" continued Claire.

"Felisa," Beverly told her with a weak smile. "After her great, great, great-grandmother Felisa Walker—the doctor on the first northern ice cap expedition to Mars."

"I read about her once, in *Martian Medicine*."

"*Martian Medicine?*" echoed T'Kavar, as she casually slipped into the seat next to Claire. "Is that still required reading?"

Beverly hadn't noticed the three first-year cadets who suddenly stepped up to the table. Two of the three—

1995

roommates Imto Partigle and Dewley Breech—were breathless. Beverly had no doubt they were pressed to keep up with their slender, long-legged companion, the Vulcan T'Kavar.

"No, don't worry, T'Kavar," replied Beverly, sighing. "Claire and I were just talking over past lives."

"Whose past life?" said Imto, eagerly. The Arcturan was suddenly interested in continuing the conversation. Beverly thought Imto wanted to talk so he could catch his breath. But then again, like most Arcturans, she knew he had an intense curiosity about everything. She smiled as she remembered their first class together. Imto's hand was always in the air to raise a point or ask a question. Physically, the Arcturan was small, with light skin that contrasted with his black and white streaked, curly hair. He had high cheekbones and a pointed chin. But it was his large, coal-black eyes capped by white, fuzzy eyebrows that everyone first noticed.

And where there was Imto, there was usually his roommate, Dewley Breech. He was tall and thin, and the thick mass of freckles across his face seemed to match his short red hair. Beverly liked Dewley's infectious smile—and that he seemed to know something about everything. One minute he could talk to you about the intricacies of warp drive, then switch to which team won the baseball World Series on Earth in the year 2014.

"Well, our present lives won't be too good if we don't get going," Dewley pointed out. He reached into his pocket for his assignment padd, his fingers flying across the computer's flat control panel. He checked the read-out on the small screen. "Next stop: Terran Anatomy

7

class. We're supposed to identify all the bones of a three-dimensional human skeleton."

"And I suppose you know all the parts already?" inquired T'Kavar, her upswept eyebrows creeping even higher as she looked at Dewley.

He smiled at the dark-haired Vulcan. "Of course," he replied in a tone that implied there was no doubt. He turned to Beverly and Claire. "And did you two remember that class starts ten minutes early today? In other words, three point six minutes from now?"

Beverly stood up and walked toward the recyclator. She turned to see Imto and Dewley walk quickly out of the cafeteria behind T'Kavar. As first-year Starfleet Medical cadets, they followed certain rules and regulations. One rule included not running to class or anywhere else. If an upperclassman caught a first-year cadet running, the result would be a quick speech—what the upperclassmen called the "warp drive" lecture. If an instructor caught an overly swift cadet, the cadet received a long speech that Dewley once labeled the "impulse drive" lecture.

With no regret, Beverly watched as her half-finished plate of Gringle Dash disappeared in the recyclator. Claire placed her tray in the recyclator and leaned toward her roommate. "Well, Bev," she whispered, "are you with me?"

Beverly absently pulled on her lower lip, deep in thought. She knew they shouldn't skip class. But Claire was right: They had studied Terran Anatomy for the past three days and knew all the bones in the human body. Actually because she knew she wanted to study medicine

Beverly had learned all the bones of the human skeleton years ago—on her own.

She also liked the idea of being one of the first to view the latest artifacts in the Old San Francisco archaeological dig. Plus, they *were* skipping class to further their education. Her grandmother would certainly approve of learning more about medicine.

"Oh, all right," Beverly said with a tight smile. "If I don't go with you, you'll probably get into trouble."

"That's the Bev I know," responded Claire. She put her arm around Beverly's shoulders as they started walking out of the cafeteria.

Beverly swallowed hard and hoped her afternoon would be better than her morning.

CHAPTER

2

Beverly would never grow tired of walking through the Academy grounds. The Presidio, as the Academy grounds were called, was built on the old military base of the same name. She once read about the old base: Large barracks held rows of beds for the military personnel. Old homes were converted to accommodate officers. And long warehouses stored military equipment.

But the grounds no longer held barracks, old homes, or warehouses. It now housed the classrooms and dorms of the top training academy in the Federation: Starfleet Academy.

Beverly remembered the orientation lecture her first week at the Academy. The ensign who guided the new cadets around the campus explained how the Presidio was surrounded by many famous sites: To the north was one of the oldest standing monuments to remarkable engineering—the Golden Gate Bridge. To the east and south was the busy and bustling city of San Francisco. And to the west was the constant, crashing surf of the deep blue Pacific ocean.

The campus grounds added to the natural and technological wonders of the San Francisco area. Beverly wasn't used to being surrounded by the leading edge of science—most of the colonies on which she lived had a minimum of Federation technology. She was becoming comfortable with the many gadgets, transporters, and shuttles, but often thought her grandmother would not like life at the Academy. She would probably wonder where to find her herbs. And she would definitely question the funny wand in Beverly's pocket—the medical scanner that all medical cadets were given on their first day at the Academy.

The Academy buildings were all light gray—almost a perfect color match to the structures at the nearby United Federation of Planets' grounds in San Francisco. Beverly was particularly fascinated by the south-facing white solar collectors that capped the campus buildings. The ensign explained that microcells within the collectors gathered energy from the sun for lighting, heating and cooling, and replicator power throughout the buildings.

And of course, the ensign had added, the climate was controlled. Finding enough sunlight to run the solar collecting microcells was not a problem.

Cutting between the grays and whites of the buildings were a crisscross of walkways lined with tall trees and gardens of colorful flowers. The hardy plants were not only from Earth, but also from Earth-like planets. Beverly recognized yellow and orange marigolds and tall, deep red hollyhocks from Earth. Blue Spinners from Granamy sang as they moved in the slight breeze; and the thin fronds of the Foggy Ferns from Ceres II looked misty in the sunlight.

As they walked by a row of white and pink dahlias, Beverly suddenly felt the natural coolness of water. Looking down, she saw a small trickle of water cutting through the garden at her feet. Following the water's path with her eyes, she noticed it led to the larger stream that ran under a wooden bridge in the distance. Since coming to the Academy, she'd visited the bridge often, relaxing as she listened to the stream's soft babble.

I bet the Presidio was just as beautiful in the twenty-first century, Beverly thought. At least until a major earthquake struck the area, tearing the city apart.

In order to get to the archaeological dig, Beverly and Claire walked across a wide path to the southeast end of the Presidio. Beverly expected the dig to be a large hole in the earth. She was amazed when it looked more like a cave than a hole.

The cadets watched as people dressed in light blue coveralls walked in and out of the cave, many carrying artifacts to set on long tables just outside the dig. "Look, Bev," said Claire, grabbing Beverly's shirtsleeve and pulling her close to a nearby table. "That looks like a . . . a stethoscope!"

Beverly leaned closer to the corroded disk. "It's a little crumbly, but I think that round disk is what they used to listen to the pulse and heart."

"And there's a hypodermic needle," Claire added. She pointed to a dirty tube with a needle at one end. "They actually inserted the needle end into a patient to give them medicine."

Beverly shuddered. "Thank goodness for hyposprays."

"Can I help you?" said a voice. Beverly turned and straightened. A Starfleet lieutenant commander stood behind the cadets, a quizzical look on her face. Beverly imagined that it was probably rare to see medical cadets at an archaeological dig.

"Oh, yes. I'm Cadet Claire Voy," Claire said smoothly. She held her hand out to the officer. "And this is Cadet Beverly Howard." She motioned to her roommate. "Starfleet Medical."

"I'm Lieutenant Commander Grisik from Starfleet Archeology and Anthropology or A&A as we call it," she said with a smile. She shook both cadets' hands. Her dark hair was short and her blue eyes matched her coveralls.

"We heard the hospital was being opened up today," Claire continued. "We just wanted to—well, be here for the excitement."

Beverly thought the officer looked slightly nervous as she quickly scanned the dig. "I know what you mean. I didn't sleep a wink last night thinking about today's dig. Are you both here to help?"

Before Beverly could say anything, Claire answered, "Sure." Beverly tried to smile, but it was more like a grimace. She knew how Claire had talked her into coming to the dig. Now she wondered how Claire had talked her into *joining* the dig.

"Good. There's a replicator over there. Just order some coveralls and gloves. Believe me, you'll need

them," she said, holding up her dirty gloves to show the cadets.

Beverly glared at Claire as they ordered, and then struggled into the coveralls. She wanted to tell Claire that she had gone too far this time. But before she could comment to her roommate, an ensign waved them into the opening of the cave. As they put on their gloves, they stepped down several small metal stairs and into the dig.

Beverly looked around and whistled. The cave was deeper than she expected, reaching back about one hundred yards from the opening. Bright white light bathed the far end of the dig as workers took holo-images of the fresh cave-in opening. Nearby, sparks flew as an A&A officer used a large laser cutter to slice into a chunk of metal protruding from the wall. Tricorders whirred as several workers recorded each artifact. As Beverly and Claire walked to the far end of the roomy cave, they saw artifacts everywhere—in the walls, on the floor, and even sticking out from the ceiling.

Grisik was already there. She was using a handheld laser cutter to gently scrape dirt from a metal box stuck in a side wall. "Welcome to the dungeon," she said, smiling as she worked on the thick object. "We're working on the basement of the hospital. Get one of the laser cutters and help me cut out this package. It's hard to read the side of the box, but I think it says something about wooden tongue depressors. Hopefully, the package is well sealed—we might find some that haven't decayed."

"Tongue depressors," muttered Beverly, as she walked over to the nearby equipment bay. "I'm skipping class for tongue depressors?" Claire smiled and nodded. Beverly grinned back sarcastically at her roommate. The cadets each picked up a laser cutter and turned to help Grisik.

By watching the lieutenant commander, Beverly soon figured out how to extract an artifact from the dirt. She pushed the wall with her gloved fingers, testing the hardness of the dirt. Setting the laser cutter on low allowed her to gently cut through loose sections of the wall. A higher setting would cut through the more solid, compacted dirt.

It was slow work. As she peeled off layer after layer of dirt, Beverly suddenly saw the tip of a shiny object. Slowly cutting away the dirt, she found what looked like two long metal sticks hinged together in the middle. The metal was shaped into wide ovals on the ends of both sticks. Beverly smiled as Grisik announced her first real find: a pair of operating room scissors.

Beverly was soon fascinated—not only by the many artifacts, but with the story that Grisik told as they worked. The officer explained how an earthquake measuring 7.8 on the Richter scale struck the area in 2036, virtually leveling much of San Francisco. As Beverly helped her cut through several layers of dirt around another object, Grisik further explained how the structural supports in twenty-first century buildings differed from modern buildings.

"By the twenty-second century," continued the lieutenant commander, "we developed billerite—the building material that absorbs the shake of an earthquake measuring up to 6.5 on the Richter scale. And now we regulate the larger earthquakes with special satellites orbiting the Earth. But back then, even the smaller tremors would crack buildings. So when the big quake came—"

"The city was in ruin," finished Beverly.

Grisik nodded. She further explained that after the quake, the city officials decided to bury most of the old city and build a new city on top. Fewer roads were rebuilt throughout the city and new building regulations were proposed to lessen the damage from future large quakes. Beverly knew about one of those rules from her reading: For close to a century after the quake, no structure built in San Francisco could be more than three stories high.

"We had some trouble finding this hospital. We had maps of the old city. But all the large and small quakes in the past two centuries managed to shift many buildings and parts of the land into different positions," Grisik pointed out. "We were lucky. One of our academy students in A&A found part of a hospital sign after yesterday's cave-in. And as you can see, the laser cutters did the rest to clear out some debris."

Beverly half listened as Grisik and Claire continued to talk about old medical equipment. But something was bothering her. Pulling out broken objects and talking about the devastating earthquake brought back memories.

Beverly suddenly shivered. It reminded her of the disaster on Arvada III.

She and her grandmother moved to Arvada III to help with the new Federation colony. By the time they arrived, over two-hundred-thousand colonists were scattered across the two large continents—all there with the promise of colonizing the new world.

Beverly remembered the planet's nighttime sky the most: two bright and beautiful moons passing one another night after night—the deeply-fractured, small moon always outpacing the bigger moon in their constant spins around the planet. The scientists took readings of the moons, noted their composition, and then turned their attention to colonizing Arvada III.

One short Arvada-year after Beverly and her grandmother arrived, the moons went astray. They came closer together in their orbit, as they had done for hundreds of thousands of years before the colonists arrived. But this time, the gravitational tug of the larger moon pulled off a piece of the fragile, smaller moon. In two more orbits around the planet, the one-mile-wide rock flew into the path of Arvada. It smashed into the shallow ocean, sending water, steam, and dust high into the planet's atmosphere.

Soon clouds and dust filled the sky, blocking the sunlight for weeks. Streams and rivers swelled as the teeming rain saturated the ground. Water tore through towns and broke through natural dams in the rivers. The winds increased, blowing many homes apart and causing ocean waves to tear away long stretches of towns along the shorelines. It was as if a hundred hurricanes suddenly hit the land and sea—all at once.

The medical supplies ran out first. Beverly remembered her grandmother's small figure covered with mud and rain as she searched the still-standing woods nearby. She would look for herbs and roots, then tend the injured with the planet's natural cures.

Smaller Starfleet vessels closest to the planet brought some food and medicine, but they could not supply every town and city. It took almost a month before enough ships could reach the planet and rescue all the colonists. During that time, Beverly learned the hard way about roots and herbs—and how to use them for food and medicine.

It was then, too, that she told herself, if she made it out alive, she would devote her life to helping others to survive.

"Heads up! Out! Now!"

The shouting shook Beverly from her thoughts. She looked around and saw a Starfleet captain yelling orders. One of the walls was quickly collapsing—and just as fast, a containment field shimmered into view to hold back the dust and debris.

But the containment field was not fast enough. A strong, pungent odor quickly filled the cave. Even though the air filters were activated, several people coughed violently as they ran away from the latest cave-in.

The red and white emergency lights turned on as the bright lights flicked and went out. "Come on!" Grisik yelled, quickly turning and pushing the cadets toward the cave opening. Beverly dropped her laser cutter and ran, with Grisik and Claire following close behind.

As she ran, Beverly covered her mouth and nose with a cloth she had in her coveralls. It was easy to follow the line of the emergency lights, but the uneven floor made it difficult to run. Claire tripped once and grabbed Beverly for support. Beverly was wishing for a strong flashlight when she finally saw the light of the cave opening.

Beverly was first to run up the metal stairs and reach

the outside. She turned around and braced herself against the outside wall. Reaching out, she pulled people up the stairs as fast as possible. Several times, she felt as if her arm would be pulled out of its socket. Some workers were coughing as she pulled them up; others were covering their mouths and noses with a cloth or their shirtsleeves.

In a few minutes, everyone was out of the cave. Beverly leaned back and let out a sigh of relief—and tried to stop her heart from racing.

The news of the latest cave-in traveled fast. Beverly jumped when she heard the hum of transporters, and suddenly Starfleet medical and emergency personnel were everywhere. Beverly watched with interest as a doctor checked her with a medical tricorder. As she looked around the crowd at the opening of the cave, she spotted Claire. She nodded to her roommate, indicating that she was all right. Claire nodded back.

Beverly overheard the captain tell the lieutenant commander to proceed with decontamination. His tricorder had indicated that the gas was probably from the hospital garbage—and he and the two officers closest to the cave-in should be checked. As the officers disappeared in the shimmer of the transporter on their way to Sickbay Four, Grisik ordered everyone to remove their dirty gloves and coveralls. As Beverly and Claire slipped off their overclothes, a special bin was transported to the area to hold the clothes for decontamination.

"Great," Grisik moaned as she dropped her coveralls in the bin next to Beverly. "We were trying to develop a holodeck simulation of the hospital. Looks like we

21

have to postpone that for a while. And here comes the commander in charge of the simulation."

Beverly turned around and gasped. She recognized the muscular, blond officer heading in their direction: It was Commander Max Wiley, the professor who taught her holodeck simulation course, Medical Emergencies. In fact, Beverly thought with a shiver, he was *the* Max Wiley, one of the toughest professors at the Academy. She was afraid her jaw was hanging open.

"Oh, no," Beverly heard Claire whisper.

"Over here, Commander," called Grisik, waving to the officer. She sighed deeply as he approached. "Sir, we were just taking holo-images when part of the west wing caved again. It's behind a containment field right now. But we won't be able to get back inside for a few hours."

Wiley nodded and said nothing.

"Oh, and Commander," she said, turning to Beverly and Claire. "We don't get many cadets from Starfleet Medical asking to help with a dig. And these two cadets were very helpful—before and after the cave-in."

Wiley turned to the cadets and folded his arms across his broad chest. "Cadets Howard and Voy? Both first-year cadets," he said.

They both stiffened. Grisik looked stunned.

"Most first-year cadets I know have a class at this time of the day," he continued.

"Well, we—" Beverly started to say.

"You what, Cadet Howard?" pressed Wiley. He leaned closer. She resisted the urge to lean back. "You aren't in class. You are here. You skipped class. Am I right?"

Beverly nodded and Claire looked down at the ground.

"Which class?"

"Terran Anatomy, sir," answered Beverly, feeling her face flush.

"This is unbecoming a Starfleet cadet," Wiley said sternly. Beverly cringed as he added, "Both of you—come with me. We're going to pay the Commanding Officer of Starfleet Medical a visit."

Beverly realized her afternoon *was* turning out to be worse than her morning.

CHAPTER

3

The two cadets remained silent as they walked behind Commander Wiley. Beverly easily kept up with the officer's long strides. But she noticed Claire was having trouble keeping pace.

Beverly felt as if they had been walking for hours. But in reality, it only took about ten minutes to reach their destination. As Wiley accompanied a senior cadet into the Commanding Officer's office, the roommates sat down in the two stiff, brown chairs decorating the room. *Obviously, the C.O. does not want people to camp out in her waiting room,* Beverly mused.

Neither Beverly or Claire spoke for a while. In a way, Beverly was mad at Claire for convincing her to go to the dig, but she was madder at herself for saying yes. Finally, Claire sighed, leaned her head back, and stared at the ceiling. "Does it seem like we've been here for hours?"

"Days," answered Beverly. She crossed her long legs and looked at the chronoclock on the wall. "But it's only been ten minutes."

"Ten minutes?" asked Claire. She frowned and shook her head. "It only takes two nanoseconds to press the computer authorization to throw us out of Starfleet Medical."

Beverly closed her eyes and crossed her arms. In the entire time they had been walking to the C.O.'s office, she'd never thought of being thrown out of Starfleet. Probation, maybe. Thrown out, never. She might be homesick, but if she was going to leave Starfleet, she wanted it to be her own decision. How would she explain her sudden arrival back home to her grandmother? What would she tell her friends who had been so excited that she was headed for Starfleet Academy? And she wondered what she would tell herself.

Beverly felt Claire jump as Commander Wiley walked briskly out of the C.O.'s office. He frowned at both cadets. Without a word, he walked out the door.

They both stood up as the senior cadet reentered the room. "Admiral Muti will see you now. Please follow me."

Admiral Muti's office was one of the most neat, spacious—and beautiful—Beverly had ever seen. Spotlights shined on works of art along several of the walls. She recognized Klingon symbols on a bronze statue and Betazoid script on two separate stone sculptures. There were also framed prints by Earth artists, including Claude Monet and Leonardo da Vinci, hanging on the wall in the far corner.

Even the windows look like art, Beverly thought.

25

Through a big bay window, Beverly could see the northern view of the Academy grounds. In the distance were the red Golden Gate Bridge and blue waters of the Pacific. Lush, green vines with colorful flowers circled the window and added to the view.

Along one wall, a mural sparkled with color. It hummed a pleasant tone as she walked to the middle of the room. She noticed that Claire was staring at the wall, too—almost as if she were spellbound by the shimmering artwork.

"Do you know what that is, Cadet?" came the admiral's low, resonant voice.

Beverly was instantly aware of the admiral. The officer stood next to a tall chair behind a large wooden desk. Her short, curly white hair contrasted with her dark, thin face. And even though she was of medium height, she suddenly seemed to dominate the entire room.

"Yes," responded Claire with a slight smile. "It's an art-harp from Niriad. In the Victorian star system."

The admiral nodded once. Her face seemed to soften slightly, then became stern again. "I am Admiral Muti, the Commanding Officer at Starfleet Medical," she told them. Her gaze never wavered from the cadets. "And you are both first-year Starfleet Medical cadets?"

The cadets came to stiff attention. "Yes, sir," they replied in unison.

"Cadets Beverly Howard and Claire Voy." She looked down at a small data padd in her hand. "Both born in Copernicus City, Luna. Interesting. And now roommates."

Beverly tried to stop her heart from beating so fast. She shifted her feet and stared straight ahead at the wall

behind the admiral. The statements didn't seem to need
an answer.

"Beverly Howard. First-year Starfleet Medical cadet.
On tests, you qualified as an honors student before you
entered Starfleet Academy. And you played the lead in
several musicals and plays. Dancing? Singing?"

"A little of both, sir, but mostly dancing . . . sir," she
stammered.

"Commendable, Cadet. It shows a presence in front
of others," she said. She pressed another template on
the padd. "Claire Voy. Also a first-year Starfleet Medical

27

cadet. And an honors student, too. You are an expert tennis player?"

"I ... I was going to be a professional tennis player, but then I decided I wanted to be a doctor instead ... sir," Claire said, reddening when she realized she had probably said too much.

Muti cleared her throat and snapped the padd shut. "I also understand, from what Commander Wiley told me, that you both were at the archaeological dig this afternoon instead of attending Terran Anatomy class. Is this correct?"

"Yes, sir," they replied, still at attention.

Muti walked past the desk and stood in front of the cadets. "Do you know why you were both chosen to attend Starfleet Academy? I'm sure you do," she said, before either cadet could reply. "You received some of the top marks in the Starfleet Medical entrance exams. You were level-headed in emergencies. And you were committed to learning."

She paused and walked around the cadets.

"And perhaps I should reinforce the philosophy of Starfleet Medical. It stresses the responsibility of the doctor to the patient—on all worlds," she emphasized. "But you know that, too, don't you? Now let me reinforce *your* responsibility to Starfleet Medical: Be the best doctors you can be for your patients. And that means being responsible by attending all your classes and understanding what is taught to you in those classes. Am I making myself clear?"

Beverly and Claire nodded and murmured, "Yes, sir."

"You may not believe that the class you skipped was important. But every class at the Academy is important.

Let me give you an example," she said, as she again stood in front of the cadets. "Say you're on the planet Epsilon Five and a person needs your help. She has a certain medical condition that you can't identify. Why? Because maybe the class you skipped had that one piece of information you needed to understand the patient's condition. Maybe it was something the professor said or a question another cadet asked that day. Maybe that one bit of information was the piece of the medical puzzle you were looking for—so you could save the patient's life," Muti stressed. "But you don't know the answer because you weren't in class."

Beverly tried to concentrate on the wall behind the admiral, but the officer's dark eyes seemed to draw her in.

"I've seen your records," continued Muti, lowering her voice. "You're both exemplary students. You both have a wonderful sense of duty to other people. And by being here, you have impressed upon us that you really want to become Starfleet Medical doctors. Here at the Academy, we'll help you become some of the best medical officers in the Federation. But you also have to give something back—by following the rules so we can help you become the best medical officers in the Federation."

The room was so quiet Beverly could hear Claire swallow. She knew her roommate was scared, too. *This is it,* Beverly thought. *This is where we get kicked out of the Academy.*

Muti walked toward the huge window overlooking the ocean, her hands clasped behind her back. It was a few minutes before she spoke again. "And how was it?" Muti asked over her shoulder.

"Sir?" Beverly responded. She wasn't sure what the admiral was asking.

"The dig, Cadet Howard," Muti responded. She turned around to face the cadets. "Did you see anything interesting?"

"Yes, sir, we . . . we pulled quite a few hospital artifacts from the cave while we were in there. At least until it collapsed."

"Yes, we were lucky no one was seriously hurt." Muti sighed, then looked at the stack of computer disks on her desk. "I, too, was contemplating leaving work early today to see how the new hospital dig was progressing," she said, then looked back at the cadets. "Now I don't condone what you both did. But I must add that I am pleased that you were trying to improve your knowledge by learning about the past—especially about a hospital. You're both dismissed."

Beverly froze for a second, not believing her ears. She noticed Claire was just as astounded. Both of them had expected the admiral to throw them out of the Academy or at least put them on probation.

Muti took her seat behind the desk and opened the small data padd. Beverly murmured her thanks and gently pushed Claire toward the door.

"And, cadets," said the admiral, looking up from her computer, "another slip and you're both on probation."

CHAPTER

4

Beverly awoke the next morning still thinking about their meeting with Admiral Muti. She realized the admiral was being generous. They should at least have been put on probation. Now she knew why Muti was C.O. at Starfleet Medical. She could understand both sides of a story and was fair about her judgments. *In other words, she is giving two first-year cadets another chance,* Beverly thought.

As they ate breakfast in the cafeteria, Beverly and Claire brushed up on the notes for their next class. Not that it was easy to study for Medical Ethics—there were so many philosophical ideas to work out. Beverly knew it was not like naming the bones in the body. Medical ethics dealt with interpreting the many beliefs of all the Federation cultures. *And that interpretation varied depending on your culture,* she thought.

At 0800 hours, Beverly and Claire walked into the Medical Ethics classroom—and into the middle of a conversation.

". . . I have always wanted to work on a starship as a medical officer," T'Kavar was saying. "My mother's good friend is a doctor onboard the *T'Pau*. She trained at Starfleet first, then obtained duty on the Vulcan ship."

"I'm not too sure I want to be on a starship," responded Rigellian Cadet Gren Edut, nodding slightly to the Vulcan. Beverly had met Gren well into the second week of classes. He had straight brown hair that reached his shoulders. His arms, legs, and even fingers, were long and his skin was slightly green. And even though he was broad and tall, he seemed very shy. After Beverly got to know him, he explained to her that Rigellians were taught not to talk to anyone until they had seen the person at least five times.

"Most illogical," replied the Vulcan with a straight face.

"Not really, friend T'Kavar. We have a small family compared to others on Rigel," explained Gren. "I only have a total of seventeen brothers and sisters. And since most of the Federation colonists have families, I plan on being a Starfleet doctor and take care of their children— but on solid, dry land, thank you."

"I'm sticking with computers," Dewley Breech chimed in. He turned off his computer padd and leaned back in his chair. "I would love to develop computer medical programs. Or design instruments and machines that could be used in medical labs—for use on starships *and* on the ground," he added, nodding to T'Kavar and Gren.

"I hope you don't try out your machines on your poor newts," responded Imto Partigle, referring to Dewley's collection of newts he kept in his room.

"No, but I *am* looking for volunteers," said Dewley. He smiled as he reached over and patted his Arcturan roommate on the shoulder.

Stephen Cody sat on the edge of Dewley's desk, smiling an easy smile. Beverly did not know him that well. He was a second-year Starfleet cadet training to be an officer. He and several others in the program were taking medical courses to round out their education. She also knew that his father was Starfleet Admiral Hector Cody.

"I like computers, too," Stephen was saying, "but not for use in the medical field. That's my sister's field—she's always wanted to be a space doctor."

"We're not studying to be 'space doctors,' Stephen," said Imto. "We are studying to be Starfleet doctors to help everyone *any*where."

"Yeah, right. Like I said, a space doctor," replied Stephen. He smiled at Imto. "Now what about me? Let's see. I'm like Dewley. I like computers. But I like to write programs to get rid of computer viruses in a computer—almost like the way you use vaccines in medicine to get rid of diseases in the body."

"A computer space doctor?" Imto asked.

Laughter filled the room. It ended just as quickly as the door hissed open.

Dr. Denise Camren entered the room. Everyone quickly moved to their computer stations and pressed their hands on the desk template to record their attendance in class. Dr. Camren stepped into the center of a circle of computer desks—her favorite way of teaching class.

Beverly noticed that everyone sat at attention. Like most Betazoids, Dr. Camren had dark hair and equally dark eyes, giving her a mysterious beauty that seemed to captivate everyone. As a Betazoid, she was also a telepath. But Beverly never questioned the professor's telepathic abilities. On the first day of class Dr. Camren announced, "I am not here to read your minds. I am here to *improve* your minds."

As one of the top counselors in Starfleet, Dr. Camren understood that there were many communication problems between the various cultures within the Federation. She urged the cadets to listen and better understand the diverse peoples of the galaxy—even their various fellow crewmembers on a starship. She taught them to think about the consequences of their actions, not only at the Academy, but as voyagers to other parts of the galaxy.

"Starfleet Medical does not and will never have all the answers to multispecies medicine," Dr. Camren was saying. "But our goal as medical officers is to try and understand the medical needs of as many alien races as possible—if and when they need our help.

"Let's begin with the following scenario: You are a medical doctor on a Federation starship. Suddenly, the ship is having difficulties. Several people are hurt as computer panels on the bridge explode. As a medical officer called to the bridge, is your first and foremost duty to the injured crewmembers or to help fix the damaged panels? Any comments?"

Beverly was called on as her hand went up. "If possible, a doctor should concentrate on the injured crewmembers first," she answered, "because sometimes it's only a matter of seconds to save someone's life. Not only that, others on the bridge are trained to work on the exploded panels."

"All right, I see many of you nodding your head in agreement with Cadet Howard," said Dr. Camren, turning slowly, looking at each cadet in turn. "The next scenario: Again you are a medical doctor on a Federation starship. You beam down to a planet whose culture is familiar with working and living in space, but they have never had contact with alien space travelers. You know that you cannot make contact with anyone because it would go against Starfleet's Prime Directive. While you are on the planet, you come upon an alien who was seriously ill or wounded. The problem is life-threatening and you know you can help. Would you treat the being, even if it went against Starfleet's Prime Directive?"

"You would leave the alien alone," Stephen said immediately. "The Prime Directive comes first. There's no question about that. It's been that way since my father and his father have been in Starfleet."

Beverly noticed that Imto sat up very straight in his chair. The Arcturan's face darkened as he turned and faced Stephen. "A life is more important than the Prime Directive."

No one moved. Dr. Camren cocked her head to one side, almost as if straining to listen. She turned to Stephen. "Cadet Cody. Your response?"

Stephen leaned forward in his chair and stared at Imto. In a low voice, he said, "Not if it will affect thousands—or even millions—of other lives, space doctor. If you cure this alien, it could upset the balance of that

35

culture. I understand the impulse to help, Imto, but the Prime Directive states that you can't mess with another culture if it interferes with the normal development of that culture. What if the ill alien plays a major role in their political structure? And since the culture has never seen aliens from space—how will they react to our sudden presence?"

"My people would not be here today if someone had followed the Prime Directive," Imto said in an equally low voice. "We did not know there were spacefaring beings. But we had a global medical disaster and a medical team from Starfleet helped us. If they had not believed that the patient comes first, many of my people would have died. And we would not be members of the Federation."

"Then those Starfleet officers were wrong. T'Kavar would agree with me, I think," responded Stephen. He looked toward the Vulcan cadet. "After all, it was a famous Vulcan who said, 'The needs of the many outweigh the needs of the one.' "

Imto snorted, his hands clenched in fists at his side. *"Mr. Cody,"* he emphasized, *"sayings* are words. Sentient beings are living—"

"Mr. Partigle," interrupted Stephen. "You can't put the patient first in a Prime Directive case. It interferes with the natural progress of that society. Who are we to make that decision for another planet?" He softened his voice. "Listen, Imto. Every Starfleet cadet and officer takes many oaths—but our first and foremost duty is to Starfleet and the Prime Directive."

No one moved, even as a chime signaled the end of class. Imto raised his voice above the ringing. "Wrong,

Mr. Cody. We *cannot* ignore the needs of people who need our help—"

"And Starfleet did *not* get where it is today by not following the Prime Directive, Mr. Partigle," said Stephen, raising his voice.

"As you were, cadets," Dr. Camren interrupted. A frown fell across her face as she stepped close to the two cadets. "Class is dismissed. Except Cadets Cody and Partigle."

CHAPTER

5

Beverly immediately noticed Commander Max Wiley was not happy. The reason was Dr. Camren's class went overtime—and most of his cadets were late. Beverly also knew he did *not* want to hear any excuses.

Beverly nervously shifted in her seat. Wiley's Medical Emergencies course was not easy. In each class, cadets coped with a crisis with a medical emergency thrown in—all simulated in the holodeck. And every week, the emergencies were harder to solve and occurred faster. No one knew what to expect. In one simulation, you piloted a shuttle and solved a medical emergency. In the next simulation, you fixed a leaking conduit in engineering and at the same time helped a fallen comrade. It was scary. Beverly knew that every decision she made could affect the crewmates around her. And after every class, she would ask herself the same question: Am I really Starfleet material?

But the worst part of the class was Wiley's tough attitude. Beverly remembered the first day in Wiley's class. She knew his speech to first-year cadets was always the same. "Look to the right of you," he would say. "Now look to the left of you. These people will probably not be here next year. Gone. Not good enough for Starfleet. Will it be you?"

Today's short lecture was just as stern. "May I remind you that promptness is a necessity in Starfleet," he stated, standing ramrod straight in front of the cadets, his hands clasped behind his back. "And I will add a second message. All classes must be attended. All classes are essential for the well-rounded Starfleet officer."

Even though Wiley didn't look in their direction, Beverly and Claire exchanged glances. Beverly knew the brief lecture was especially pointed at them.

Wiley moved behind the main computer console. Commander Vadoc, an instructor from Starfleet Medical, was already in place behind the computer. The Vulcan commander was in charge of choosing the holodeck simulations for the Starfleet Medical students and often helped Wiley announce each exercise.

"The first simulation team will consist of Cadets T'Kavar and Howard," announced Vadoc, reading from a computer screen. "You will be negotiating the Benthos asteroid belt. Your shuttlecraft has just entered the belt. There is an Andorian ensign in your crew. You are to head to the planet Pella beyond the belt. As usual, when you are ready to proceed with the simulation, you must both step on the template. The program will then begin."

Beverly and T'Kavar stepped up to the circular pad on the floor to begin the first simulation.

The door suddenly hissed open and Stephen Cody and Imto Partigle rushed in.

"Cadet Partigle," Wiley said scornfully. "Glad you could join us. You missed my lecture on promptness so I'll repeat it to you after class. Please sit with the rest of the cadets." Wiley turned to Stephen. "So my assistant finally made it, too. Cadet Cody, I expect you to come to an assigned class on time. You have work to do. Please take your place with me at the simulation computer."

Stephen hurried behind the console and stood next to Wiley. He gave a wan smile to the officers. "Ready to proceed on your commands, sirs."

"Please step on the circular template in the center of the room," continued Vadoc to the two waiting cadets. "You both must handle all general and medical emergencies that may arise. Begin when ready."

Beverly and T'Kavar looked at each other and nodded. As they stepped on the template, the cadet- and computer-filled room seemed to dissolve. They were suddenly onboard a Federation starship shuttlecraft. But it was the viewscreen that caught Beverly's eye—a dense collection of rocky asteroids loomed in front of the tiny craft.

A yellow alert klaxon sounded as a computer voice rang out.

"Warning. Shuttlecraft has entered the outer limits of the Benthos asteroid belt."

T'Kavar quickly sat in the left pilot seat. Her fingers flew over the computer panels controlling the shuttle's microfusion thruster units. "I will handle the shuttle," she called to Beverly. "Cutting back on the thrusters should slow us down and allow me to negotiate the belt."

"Warning. Communications have been compromised."

Beverly sat in the pilot's seat next to T'Kavar. She punched several square panels on the communications console and frowned as she read the computer readout. Communications with Starfleet and Pella were definitely down. According to the information on the screen, the mostly-metal asteroids interfered with communications. She pushed several panels to compensate for the asteroids and smiled as a red warning light above the console turned yellow.

"Communication paths restored."

There was a loud groan behind the two cadets. T'Kavar raised an eyebrow at Beverly.

"I've got it," Beverly responded, grabbing a nearby holographic medical tricorder. She hurried to the back of the shuttle. Behind the last seat was a young, blue-skinned Andorian ensign. The left antenna on his head was broken and bleeding, and his arm was bent back in an unnatural position.

"I . . . I was thrown against a bulkhead when the first asteroid hit," the ensign whispered.

"First asteroid? We were hit before—"

The craft suddenly pitched to the left. The ensign grabbed the seat with his good arm. Beverly was thrown to the ground, the medical tricorder flying from her hand. She covered her head as a side panel above her spit out sparks. She quickly looked to the front of the shuttle. T'Kavar was still in her seat, holding on to the console—a deep frown forming on her face as she concentrated on the pilot controls.

Beverly turned back to the ensign as he moaned loudly. She crawled over to him, stopping only to grab the dropped medical tricorder. Kneeling by the Andorian, she quickly ran the instrument over the ensign's body.

"You've dislocated your shoulder and you have a concussion. Just—ouch!" she yelled, grabbing her right hand and dropping the tricorder again. "It just shocked me!"

The shuttle suddenly rocked violently from side to side. As best as she could, Beverly held onto the nearby seat as a red alert klaxon began.

"Warning. Direct hit to the port thruster. Damage to propulsion systems. Evasive action recommended."

"Beverly!" T'Kavar shouted above the sound of twisting metal. "I'm trying to cut off all propulsion commands to the thrusters. Are you hurt?"

"No, I don't think so!" she yelled above the noise, looking at her throbbing hand.

"Take care of the ensign! I'll try to contact Pella or Starfleet!"

"Right!" Beverly called back, then turned to the ensign. The Andorian's face contorted in pain as he tried to move. "Just stay still," she coached in a shaky voice, "Let me see what—"

"Warning. Explosion imminent. Impulse engine overload. Explosion in three seconds . . . two seconds . . . one second . . ."

The lights dimmed. Beverly watched as the shuttlecraft and the Andorian ensign dissolved in front of her. She saw Claire, a sympathetic smile on her face. Beverly tried to smile back, but could not. Her hand tingled, and as she stood up, she felt as if she had been holding her breath during the entire simulation.

"Simulation terminated," Vadoc announced.

Wiley stepped out from behind the console. "You and your shuttlecraft just blew up, cadets," he remarked, pointing out the obvious. "Cadet T'Kavar, you must remember to rely on the autopilot more often. The onboard computers can usually maneuver faster than a Vulcan—and most other sentient beings—especially with such small objects all around you," he commented. He turned to Beverly. "Cadet Howard, my advice to you is to stabilize your patient much faster—and to practice holding on to a tricorder."

Laughter rippled through the holodeck. "Yes, sir," she

43

answered. She felt her face flush. "But sir, at one point in the simulation, I thought I felt the tricorder shock me."

"I'll check that out, cadet. Please sit down, both of you," Wiley instructed. As he moved behind the console and pushed several panels, he addressed the class. "I would like to remind everyone—it is not whether you succeed in stopping an imminent explosion or healing a patient. We are testing your reactions under various conditions. And you are learning what it's like to be in an emergency situation." Wiley hesitated, looking down at his readouts, then turned to Beverly. "Hmmm . . . I'm sorry, Cadet Howard. I see no evidence of a shock coming from your tricorder. Perhaps you twisted your hand when you fell against the seat."

Beverly nodded and looked at her hand. It still tingled. "Perhaps."

Wiley turned to Vadoc and nodded. "The next simulation team will be Cadets Voy and Peterson," continued the Vulcan commander.

Claire smiled again at Beverly as she and cadet Peter Peterson stepped up to the circular template. Beverly didn't know a great deal about the second-year medical cadet. She did know that he missed the Medical Emergencies class his first year because of a family emergency—and was taking the course this year to catch up. T'Kavar once told her that Peter was the grandson of Admiral Cartwright. Over fifty years ago, the admiral and several others planned to stop peace talks between the Klingons and the Federation by assassinating the Klingon chancellor. But the scheme didn't work. Beverly remembered that Captain James T. Kirk and some of his crew from the *U.S.S. Enterprise* discovered the plan and stopped the assassination attempt. The historic Khitomer conference continued as planned—and peace between Klingons and the Federation occurred several years later. Peter seemed determined to restore his family's name in Starfleet's future.

"You will be on a Federation starship," Vadoc was announcing, reading from the computer screen in front of him. "Cadet Peterson, you are the first officer onboard the *U.S.S. Gallant,* a fictitious Starfleet vessel. The starship has just been fired upon by a Romulan Bird-of-Prey with both phasers and photon torpedoes. Cadet Voy, you will be a lieutenant commander on the ship's medical team. You have just been called to the bridge. You both must handle all general and medical emergencies that arise. Begin when ready."

As they stepped on the template, Beverly and the other students watched as the room before them dissolved into the expansive bridge of a Federation starship. As a red alert klaxon sounded in the background, several bridge officers were pulling themselves up from the floor, trying to reach their stations. The tactical officer announced a phaser strike to decks three and four, but shields were holding. The officer at the operations center grunted and replied that the Romulan Bird-of-Prey had cloaked again. The captain acknowledged the officers' remarks, then moved quickly to navigation to help put out a small electrical fire.

Peter was helping the helmsman crawl back to his seat when Claire nudged him and pointed to the viewscreen. They both gaped as the stars seemed to ripple—and a Romulan ship uncloaked. As it flew past the *Gallant,* another phaser blast struck the Federation ship. Peter was thrown to the right, while Claire fell to the floor next to the captain.

"Doctor!" shouted the captain above the red alert klaxon. He helped Claire to her feet. "Attend to the first officer. He's over there," he said, pointing to Peter. "Helm, take us out of here—away from the Bird-of-Prey. Mark one-seven-two! Warp seven!"

Claire rushed over to Peter. His eyes were closed and he was holding his stomach. "Peter, you all right?" she asked. She grabbed a nearby holographic medical tricorder and bent down, running the instrument over him.

Peter opened his eyes wide—and started shaking uncontrollably.

"Hey, Peter," Claire whispered to him, "you're doing a good job. It looks like you're really hurt." She hesitated and smacked the side of the tricorder. "Strange. I can't seem to get a reading out of this thing."

Beverly was puzzled. She shifted uncomfortably in her chair as she watched her roommate from the side. Peter kept shaking as Claire tried to scan. He was very convincing as a patient. *In fact, too convincing,* Beverly thought.

She couldn't stand it anymore. Even though it was against class rules, she ran over and stood beside Claire. "What's wrong with Peter?" she shouted above the noise.

"Bev . . . What are you . . . It's all right, Bev, go on back," Claire protested, frowning and waving Beverly back to the side. "Peter's just playing his part of the simulation, remember?"

"I don't think so, Claire," she replied. She quickly bent down and pushed the medical tricorder away from Peter. It slipped from Claire's hand and clattered to the floor.

Beverly grimaced as the captain continued to yell commands in the background. Reaching into her jumpsuit pocket, she winced as she pulled out her small personal medical scanner with her sore hand. Peter did not move. She ran the scanner over his head and chest and announced above the noise, "He's had some type of seizure—or a shock." She reached out and took Peter's hand. It was cold and clammy. "Computer! Stop program!"

It startled Beverly as the noise quickly ceased and the starship dissolved around her. Claire knelt on the floor beside her and stared at Peter. Beverly looked up and saw the stunned faces of her classmates.

She suddenly noticed Wiley and Vadoc at her side, so she moved out of the way. Vadoc examined Peter with his medical tricorder and tapped the comm badge on his shirt. "Medical emergency. Direct transport to Sickbay Five. Two to beam over. Energize."

Everyone quietly watched as Peter and Vadoc transported out of the holodeck. Peter's face was pale and he was barely conscious. *At least he's still breathing,* Beverly thought.

As the whine of the transporter ended, Wiley turned to Claire and ran his hand through his short hair. *"What-did-you-do?"* he demanded, emphasizing each word.

Claire was dumbfounded. "Nothing, sir, I—"

"What do you mean 'nothing'?" he interrupted. "You must have done something! There are failsafes on the holodecks. No one should get hurt." He paused and seemed to collect himself. "I repeat. What did you do?"

"Nothing, I was just doing the simulation, really," Claire protested, standing up to face Wiley. "The tricorder didn't seem to work, so I—"

Beverly stood close to Wiley. "Sir, I was watching. Maybe it was the same shock that got me. I know Cadet Voy didn't—"

"I didn't ask for your opinion, Cadet Howard," he responded, glaring at Beverly. She quickly stepped back as he turned to Claire again. "Do you remember pushing a wrong button? Did you trip over anything?"

"No, sir," Claire protested, her voice cracking. "I wasn't even close to any consoles. I just went along with the simulation. What happened to Peter wasn't my fault—I mean, it couldn't be my fault."

"We'll see about that," said Wiley. He turned on his heel and marched toward the exit of the holodeck classroom.

As he approached the door, the whine of the transporter filled the now silent room. Commander Vadoc materialized and walked up to Wiley. "Commander Wiley, you best come with me. As professor, it is your responsibility for the simulations."

"Yes, I know. So let me do my job and determine what happened," said Wiley, moving past Vadoc.

"On the contrary, Commander," Vadoc said in a matter-of-fact voice, as he firmly grasped Wiley's arm. "You are to report to your Commanding Officer. One cadet—perhaps two," he said, nodding to Beverly, "has been hurt under your authority. One such incident may be considered an accident. I do not mean to imply anything, but two such incidents may be deliberate."

Wiley glared in Claire's direction. "We'll see about that, too," he growled and walked out the exit, the Vulcan commander following close behind.

CHAPTER

6

Claire looked around her dorm room and sighed. She tilted her head, puzzled. "Why didn't I see it?"

"There is no reason for you to blame yourself, Claire," said Imto Partigle, his bushy white eyebrows meeting above his nose as he frowned. "We all thought Peter's reaction was part of the simulation."

"And we still don't know what happened to Peter," added Dewley Breech, resting his hand on his chin. "Or even what happened to you, Bev. How's your hand?"

"Fine now," she responded, flexing her right hand. "Almost as if nothing happened. But I know I felt something."

Claire ignored the discussion and continued. "I should have known. I should have realized something was wrong when that dumb medical tricorder wouldn't work. Bev knew." Claire punched the pillow lying next to her in frustration.

"Claire, I was looking at the simulation from a different viewpoint," Beverly responded. She knew there was nothing she could say that would cheer Claire.

"Not only that, being in a simulation is a stimulating experience," T'Kavar pointed out as she leaned against Beverly's desk. "Things become distorted. You are not always at your best. Which is why Starfleet insists on such a class—to get us used to reacting quickly in an emergency."

"Is that supposed to make me feel better, T'Kavar?" asked Claire, narrowing her eyes at the Vulcan.

"It is the truth."

Beverly sighed and stared at the floor. They were all getting tired and testy. For the past hour, they had discussed the simulations, trying to figure out what happened. They even acted out the simulation involving Peter. Imto played the captain, T'Kavar pretended to be Claire, and Dewley acted out the part of Peter. Beverly and Claire tried to remember each move from their points of view—but to no avail. They still could not determine what happened.

The chime sounded at Beverly's door. The door hissed open and Gren Edut stepped into the room. Beverly felt as if she were waiting for the verdict from a jury.

"I talked to my friend who works in the infirmary," Gren said, standing in front of Claire and Beverly as the others gathered around him. "Peter is all right, but he's had a shock to his system. The doctors say he will not be back to school for days."

Gren further explained that Peter had been feeling ill that day, but it was only secondary to the neuroshock he received. According to the doctors, it was almost as if a strong phaser blast had hit Peter. The shock not only stunned him like a real phaser, but momentarily disrupted almost every nerve in his body. Peter's hands and feet were still numb.

"Does Peter remember anything?" asked Imto, standing next to Gren.

"No, just that he felt sick to his stomach just before class. He said he doesn't remember a thing after the simulation threw him across the bridge." Gren hesitated, lacing his long fingers in front of him. "I also heard the preliminary investigation. It showed that the holodeck did *not* malfunction."

"Does that mean it wasn't an accident?" Imto asked, scratching his head and turning to Beverly. "Could the holo-generated Andorian ensign have shocked you?"

"I don't think so, Imto," she replied. "And he wasn't present when Peter was shocked."

"And I don't think any of us believe Claire caused Peter to be shocked," added Dewley. "As far as I can see, the guilty party would have to be the person who developed the simulation—and the finger points to Wiley. But I can't figure out why he would want to hurt you or Peter."

"Maybe it was simply negligence on his part," suggested Gren.

"Or maybe he meant to hurt any one of us," replied Imto, his black eyes wide with the thought.

"There is another possibility when it comes to Peter," said T'Kavar, folding her long arms in front of her. "Peter's grandfather was involved in the conspiracy to stop the early Klingon and Federation alliance at Khitomer. I know that Wiley was on Khitomer as a third-year cadet. He was assigned to the *U.S.S. Magellan* on a training mission sent to the planet. And he has always firmly supported the Klingon-Federation alliance."

"How do you know that?" asked Dewley, staring at the cadet.

"I read a great deal."

"T'Kavar, do you think Wiley would hurt Peter because of his grandfather's involvement in trying to stop the peace?" Beverly asked, her brow coming together with concern.

"I am not accusing anyone of anything," T'Kavar replied, her expression as bland as usual. "I am pointing out another possibility. Like everyone else's suggestions, it is merely speculation on my part."

"But why hurt Beverly?" asked Dewley.

"She was not really hurt," T'Kavar said, "and perhaps her shock was delivered by mistake."

"Wiley was quick to dismiss Beverly's claim," added Imto.

Everyone in the room fell silent. Claire suddenly grabbed a jacket and walked out the door. Dewley looked at Beverly. "Want me to go after her?"

Beverly shook her head. She knew that Claire would head for the second floor of Regent Hall. She knew, too, that she wanted to do the same thing: confront Commander Wiley. She threw on her jacket and started after Claire.

She's running on enough adrenaline to supply all the cadets at Starfleet Medical—and so am I, Beverly thought as she saw her roommate in the distance. She, too, wanted to know why Wiley, or anyone else, for that matter, would want to hurt a cadet. And she wanted to know what he was hiding—why he didn't listen to her when she said she had been shocked.

She caught up with Claire as she reached the door of Regent Hall. Neither said a word as they entered the building. No one passed them as they walked up the stairs to Wiley's office. Beverly was glad that the corridors were empty. At this time of the day, some students were studying in study halls and reading centers; others were making their daily trek to the cafeteria for dinner. And still others were in their dorm rooms, using the extra time before dinner to prepare for the next day's classes.

Claire pressed the chime on Wiley's office door, but there was no answer. "Computer," she said, speaking to the computer control display on the wall. "Where is Commander Max Wiley?"

"Commander Max Wiley is currently on the first floor of Regent Hall."

The cadets looked wide-eyed at each other as the sound of footsteps rang through the stairwell. Commander Wiley appeared from around the corner and stopped. An unwelcoming smile crossed his lips.

"Wonderful. Just wonderful. First I have to deal with Muti—now you two."

"We just came to talk to you," said Claire, her shaking voice barely a whisper.

Wiley chuckled softly to himself and stepped past the cadets to open his door. "Well, you might as well come in," he said as the door swooshed opened. Beverly had never seen the commander look so despondent. Suddenly, she was worried. In the three weeks she had been attending Wiley's class, he had always stood tall. He always talked with a confidence that only comes with command. The man before her was stooped and tired. It was almost as if he didn't care about anything—almost as if he had given up.

They followed the commander into his office. Beverly looked around the room and noticed two shelves of old books and stacks of computer tapes. In front of the stacks was a large glass and metal desk. The office was just like Wiley: tidy, professional, and in perfect order.

"Commander Wiley, there is no way I could have done something wrong during the simulation—" Claire started to say.

"Yes, yes, yes," he said, throwing himself into an overstuffed chair in the corner. He threw a data padd toward his desk, but it missed and clattered to the floor. Beverly started to reach for the object. "Naw. Don't bother. Let it lie," he grunted. He turned to Claire. "Now I suppose you're going to plead with me that you did nothing wrong—that you're an outstanding student."

Claire blinked and stood up straight. "I was one of the top performers in the simulation part of the test to enter Starfleet."

"I know, Cadet Voy," responded Wiley, standing up and ordering a coffee from a nearby replicator. He picked up the steaming mug and sat down again. "I was there, remember?" he continued. "But that still doesn't mean you didn't do something wrong today."

"But what?" Claire protested.

"I have no idea—yet," he commented, pointing a finger at Claire, "but it seems this 'outstanding student' managed to skip a class yesterday. And with such disregard for the rules, why shouldn't I suspect you?"

Claire put a hand to her head and turned away from Wiley. Beverly stepped forward. "Commander Wiley, I also have a question. Why did you just dismiss the idea that I had been shocked during my simulation?"

"Because there was no evidence, Cadet Howard," he said, frowning. "You were also being thrown around the cabin of the shuttlecraft. As a future doctor, you must know that a fall can result in excessive pressure on a nerve. You probably fell just right, and it only *felt* similar to a shock."

Beverly's mouth formed a thin line in frustration. "Has anyone checked the computer simulation tape?"

she suggested. "Maybe it only seems all right. Maybe something went wrong with the tape during the simulation that caused Peter—and maybe me—to be shocked."

"Don't be ridiculous," he scoffed. "Cadet, you were not shocked. And as for the Peterson simulation, I developed it myself. And it worked perfectly before and after," he said, pointing to Claire again, "her little incident."

Claire leaned across the desk and looked Wiley in the eye. "*I* did nothing wrong."

"You must have done something wrong. Why would—" said Wiley, stopping in mid-sentence. He suddenly smiled and took another sip of coffee. "You both . . ." he started to say. He looked at Claire and Beverly in turn. "You both think I'm guilty, too," he said in a low voice, "just like everyone in Starfleet thinks I am. You think that I somehow did something to the simulation."

"Commander, none of us knows what really happened," Beverly protested.

Wiley acted as if he did not hear Beverly. She had seen that look before—a look filled with anger and bitterness. "I should have known," he whispered, "you two are trying to get me to confess to doing something to my own simulation and hurting my cadets."

He stood up and slammed his hand down on the desk. "Well, it won't work. Now get out of here!"

CHAPTER

7

Beverly was exasperated. *This is impossible,* she thought. *Peter could have died from that simulation—I could have been seriously hurt, too.* Why couldn't she convince Wiley that he was wrong—that she had been shocked, and that something was wrong with Peter's and Claire's simulation. Why didn't he see?

Claire slumped at her desk. The computer screen in front of her blinked, waiting for its next command. "I can't study," she moaned.

Beverly sighed. She knew exactly how her roommate felt. After all, her computer remained untouched for the past hour, too. "Claire, I'm exhausted. Let's try to get some rest. Think things over. Maybe things will look better in the morning."

Claire muttered in agreement. She slowly crawled under the covers as Beverly called for the computers and lights to turn off.

It wasn't easy to fall asleep. No matter what position Beverly tried, she felt uncomfortable. Why didn't Wiley want to find out the truth instead of blaming someone else for the accident?

When she last looked at the chronoclock near her bed, it was 0100 hours. She finally fell asleep and dreamed that she was trying to stop a simulation. She yelled to the computer to stop. She pushed the computer panels along a wall. But no matter what she did or said, the simulation continued. After what seemed like only a short time, she awoke in a cold sweat as an alarm chime sounded.

"Claire—time to get up," she said, throwing off the covers.

A flashing light on her comm pad caught her eye. At the same time, she noticed that Claire was not in her bed. She pressed the comm pad and Claire's face appeared on the small screen.

"Hi, Bev. I just received a message from Mrs. Oner. She said to come immediately—that she felt ill. She's helped me before, Bev, so I wanted to help her. And yes, I have permission from Ensign Linn. I'll try not to get into trouble. See you later."

Beverly quickly brushed her teeth and washed. She ordered a red and black medical cadet jumpsuit from the replicator and dressed. After brushing her hair, she looked at herself in the room's long mirror to make sure she looked neat and polished—as was expected of an Academy cadet. *The only flaw on this perfect cadet,* she thought, *is the worried look on her face.*

She looked at Claire's message on the comm pad

screen again. The time said 0410 hours. It was almost three hours since Claire had left the message.

She knocked on Ensign Linn's door and straightened the comm badge on her jumpsuit collar. Ensign Linn, the dorm's watch officer, was already dressed. "Cadet Howard," the junior class ensign said, grabbing a padd from a table near the door. "I was wondering when you would show up. You found Cadet Voy's message?"

Beverly nodded. "Yes, and I'm really surprised. I had no idea Mrs. Oner was ill. Claire usually talks quite a bit about Mrs. Oner."

"It sounded like it was pretty sudden," said Ensign Linn, handing the padd to Beverly. She pushed her left thumb on the padd, registering her thumbprint as identification. "I'll give you a pass for two hours off campus," said Linn, punching the times into the computer. "It will allow you to skip your study period this morning. If you're not back in two hours, I'll call you on your comm badge. If you still don't report within ten minutes of that time, I'll have to put you on report."

Beverly nodded. "I've never been to Mrs. Oner's—I just take Lyon to Parker Street, right?"

"Yes, you can't miss it once you're on Parker. And, Cadet," she added as Beverly turned to go, "I didn't mention this to Cadet Voy. But if you don't mind, please let me know what happens," she said, her voice softening. "In my four years at the Academy, I can't tell you how many times I visited Mrs. Oner's café. And I'm worried about her. She's . . . well, she's just very special."

It was only the second time that Beverly had been off campus since she arrived at the Academy. The first was

59

to visit her grandmother's friend the first week of school. But it didn't feel as if she was really off campus. After all, the woman's home was just across the street from the Academy grounds.

As Beverly walked, she almost forgot about yesterday's troubles. She became lost in listening to the early morning noises of the city: Overhead trams took workers to their jobs in the city. Store doors hissed open for the day. There were also street vendors from several Federation planets laying out their wares—cloth, trinkets, and gemstones that tourists liked to purchase. Long rows of neat one-story homes lined several of the streets.

She stopped once to watch several groups of children playing in a schoolyard in the early morning sunshine.

Beverly sighed. If she closed her eyes, she would have sworn this was Arvada III at its peak.

As she rounded a corner, the front window of a nearby building caught her eye. It was a florist, and there, sitting in the window, was a vase filled with very wide white and deep pink flowers. She stared at the flowers before she continued on—they were camellias, her grandmother's favorite.

Ensign Linn was right, Beverly thought. It was not hard to find Mrs. Oner's. The converted one-story home stood out from the rest of the houses on the street. It was painted pastel yellow, with rusty-red shutters that matched the stone slab shingles on the roof. Beverly thought the old building looked like a house that was popular during the late twenty-first century in San Francisco. A large white sign displayed the café's name in bright red letters: "Mrs. Oner's."

The sign in the front door window read Closed. Beverly peeked in, then knocked. Claire's face suddenly appeared. "Bev, you found me," she said, laughing as she opened the wooden door. It was the first time Beverly had seen her laugh in two days. *I haven't been laughing much in the last two days, either,* she thought.

"You're just in time," said Claire. She led Beverly around the wooden tables of the café and into the kitchen. "Mrs. Oner is making some strange concoction—and I'm trying to convince her to tell me what it is."

"But I thought she was sick."

"I had to think of some way to get off campus without

getting in trouble," Claire said sheepishly. "I just had to talk to Mrs. Oner about the problem with Commander Wiley."

Beverly took a deep breath as she entered the kitchen. The air was mixed with the most wonderful smells. She identified nutmeg, cinnamon, and cloves. Suddenly she smelled yumatia, a sweet spice from Betazed. Then fridd, from a Andorian bean that is often used as a coffee substitute. She sighed happily, suddenly feeling comfortable in the big house.

"Ah, Beverly. Come in. You're hungry," said a voice near the old style kitchen stove.

"Who wouldn't be, with all these smells," Beverly said under her breath as she turned toward the voice.

Mrs. Oner's features were soft, like her voice. She was tall and willowy, and her long arms easily reached into a cupboard for a handful of red leaves. Dropping the bunch of herbs into a shiny pot in front of her, she turned to Beverly and smiled. Her eyes were deep sky blue and she had a ruddy complexion, as if she had just scrubbed her face. *Probably from always standing over those steaming pots,* Beverly thought.

Mrs. Oner turned back to the stove. "Ah, no, Beverly, all my people have such a complexion," she said. "It is probably from being outside collecting our herbs and spices in the bright sunshine. We have two suns in our solar system, you know."

Beverly just stared at the older woman.

Mrs. Oner smiled again. Her wavy black hair fell around her face as she sniffed the contents of the pot. "Ready for breakfast? We were waiting for you."

"Yes, thank you. I . . . I haven't had breakfast yet. I

came right over from campus," stammered Beverly, realizing Mrs. Oner seemed to know that already, too.

"And how is Ensign Linn? Tell her not to worry—tell her I am fine," she said, her ankle-length pastel blue dress swaying back and forth as she turned off the stove's burners.

Beverly nodded. She realized she hadn't even mentioned Ensign Linn.

"And how did you like the camellias at the local florists? Your grandmother's favorite, right?" said Mrs. Oner. She brought the steaming pot over to the wide table in the middle of the room.

"Did you tell her that?" asked Beverly, whispering to Claire.

Her roommate shrugged her shoulders and shook her head. "Not me."

This time Mrs. Oner laughed. It was a deep, pleasant sound that made Beverly and Claire start laughing, too. Beverly didn't know why. Mrs. Oner's laugh was definitely infectious.

"Ah, Beverly," she said, ladling spoonfuls of the breakfast into three bowls. "I am from the planet Muldan. We are . . . what do you call us, Claire?"

"Touch-empaths," explained Claire. She moved over to the stove and stirred the contents of a smaller, copper-colored pan. "They understand how people feel just by touch. But Mrs. Oner is also slightly telepathic. She can tell things about people just by being near them."

"I prefer that you think of me as a friend, Beverly," Mrs. Oner replied. "Come, sit down, both of you."

Beverly enjoyed the smells of the cooking herbs and spices. She also liked the taste of the breakfast porridge

Mrs. Oner called "yebba." For a moment, Beverly felt homesick again. *The warmth, the smells, and the laughter—it's just like being back at my grandmother's house,* she thought.

Soon the conversation turned to the problem with the simulation and Commander Max Wiley. "Ah, and so you believe that Claire is not guilty of doing anything wrong," Mrs. Oner was saying, "and Commander Wiley is guilty."

"I know Claire didn't do anything during her simulation," responded Beverly, putting her spoon down. "And as for Commander Wiley? I don't know. I *do* know that I was also shocked during my simulation, but Wiley seems to deny that it could happen. He says I just fell on my hand. And then there are other things that point to the commander." She explained to the older woman why all the evidence pointed to Wiley—even mentioning T'Kavar's idea about Wiley and his connection with Khitomer. "But why would he want to hurt us?"

"Ah, Beverly," said Mrs. Oner. "It is difficult to say what leads people to hurt others. But tell me. Do you really believe Commander Wiley could do such a thing?"

"He *is* very demanding of his students and extremely stern," she responded, still looking into the older woman's eyes.

"That was not my question. Do you believe Commander Wiley could do such a thing?" asked the older woman again.

Beverly frowned and thought for a moment. "He's definitely a hard teacher. And he's not exactly warm and personable—but, no, I don't think he would harm any of his cadets. I think he treats his students sternly because he's so dedicated to Starfleet. He's trying to set an example. He wants us to be dedicated, too."

Mrs. Oner tilted her head. "And?"

"And I've tried hard," Beverly said, sighing, "but I really can't imagine him hurting one of his cadets—even if that person did remind him of Khitomer. If he did hurt someone, I think it would be an accident. He would confess that he made a mistake and pay the consequences." Beverly looked down at her empty bowl. "I don't know why I feel that way about the commander. It's . . . well, it's just a feeling I have."

"Sometimes feelings are the best way to determine the truth."

Claire reluctantly agreed. "I guess I can see that, too, even though he still blames me," she said, shifting in her chair. "After all, why would someone who loves Starfleet so much do something to get themselves kicked out?"

No one spoke. The small pot on the stove popped and bubbled. Mrs. Oner stood up and went to the stove. As she slowly stirred the pot, she looked at Beverly. There was a quizzical look on her smiling face. "Please explain to me. Everyone is checking the holodeck computer for an obvious problem," she said in her soft voice. "How about determining if the computer program was tricked—would it not show a mistake if you ran it again?"

The cadets stared at Mrs. Oner, then at each other. "I suppose so—don't you think so, Bev?" asked Claire.

"Maybe," Beverly replied. "We tried acting it out. We never asked about running the actual program. Wiley *said* it worked after our accident. But maybe it's time we did it ourselves—without Wiley around."

"Oh, no," Claire cried. "Does that mean we have to get the tape from Wiley?"

"No. We have someone else on our side—Dewley Breech. Come on," said Beverly, standing up and grabbing Claire by the arm. "Thanks, Mrs. Oner. I hate to eat and run. But we have to get back to campus and start our own investigation."

CHAPTER

8

Beverly and Claire practically ran all the way back to campus. After signing in and reassuring Ensign Linn that Mrs. Oner was all right, they headed directly to Dewley Breech's room.

Imto Partigle is a very patient person, Beverly thought as she entered Dewley's and Imto's quarters. Imto's roommate had aquariums everywhere—all making bubbling noises like the pots on Mrs. Oner's stove. Close to the farthest wall sat two large and three small aquariums. Each glass container was half-filled with water, lined with rocks and tall grasses, and contained a colorful assortment of Dewley's favorite creatures: newts. Dewley once told Beverly he had been collecting newts for years— and taking care of the tiny creatures led him into the field of medicine.

Imto popped up from behind one of the larger aquariums and grinned. "Welcome, fellow cadets, to a room filled with newts!" he exclaimed. The Arcturan bowed slightly in their direction. "We have grasses. We have rocks. And in between, we have little red, yellow, and black newts. We even have my favorite—the tiny sputted red newt."

"That's red-spotted newt!" yelled Dewley from behind an aquarium in the corner.

"Oh, right," Imto continued, bowing toward Dewley. "Red-sputted newt."

Dewley walked to the center of the room and shook his head. Smiling at his roommate, he carefully pronounced the name of the newt again. *"Red-spotted newt."*

Imto shrugged his thin shoulders. "Oh, whatever. I still don't know why you like such small creatures, Dewley. On Arctura, our 'newts' are at least three feet long. And they glow in the dark."

Beverly smirked at Imto. "Remind me to watch where I walk on Arctura."

Dewley picked up one of the red-spotted newts and held it close to Beverly. "Here's my favorite. I wanted to name him Max Wiley, but Imto wouldn't let me. So I call him Sniff." She leaned toward the small, wet creature, putting her finger close to the animal's face. It sniffed at her finger, but showed little interest. Seemingly bored with the human female, it crawled up Dewley's arm to his shoulder. "It thinks I'm a rock," said Dewley.

"Dewley, I like your newts—and Sniff. But I really came by to ask you a favor." Beverly explained to the two roommates about the confrontation with Wiley, and Mrs. Oner's suggestion to check the simulation tape for

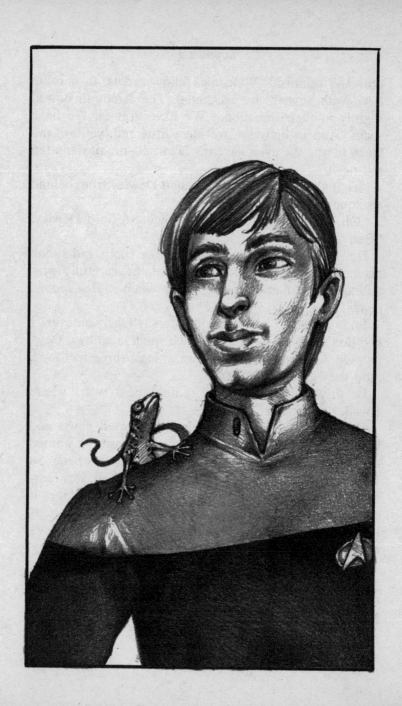

tampering. "Do you think we can get a copy of the tape from that day?"

Dewley shrugged. "It's kept in the main computer room in Regent Hall," he answered. "I don't have clearance to get the tapes. Why don't you ask Wiley?"

Claire winced and Beverly shook her head. "No, we're conducting our own investigation. And anyway, I don't think he'd cooperate. Dewley, we really have to find out if there is any evidence of tampering with the computer simulation. I want to find out if I did get a shock to prove I'm not crazy—but I also want to clear Claire." *And maybe Wiley,* she thought.

"So you want me to break into the main computer archives?" replied Dewley, his eyes becoming wide with realization.

"Not really break into the archives. Just copy a tape."

Dewley thought for a moment, then grinned. "Well, if you must know, you can't always fool a computer expert like myself," he said. He lowered his voice and leaned conspiratorially toward Beverly and Claire. "I *do* know how to get into the main computer center, but no one is supposed to know that I know."

"And of course," said Imto, smiling and standing next to his roommate, "you will need a lookout at the door."

Dewley put Sniff back into the aquarium. He pulled out a data padd and started to assign duties. Beverly thought his mannerisms were much like a doctor preparing his associates for a major operation. "Okay, Imto," he said, pressing a panel on his data padd, "you'll be the lookout. Claire, you'll do the initial search for the tape in the stacks. And Beverly, you're now our speed reader. You find the right file as the data flashes on the screen. I'll work out the codes to cover our tracks and download the tape."

The operation was ready to begin.

No one suspected the four first-year cadets—complete with data padds—walking down a hallway at Regent Hall's computer center, the focus of computer activity at the Academy. It was close to lunchtime, when few cadets were in the computer building. Dewley talked casually to Imto, discussing computer codes and newts. Claire just smiled weakly at Beverly now and then.

They entered the outer study hall of the main computer room. Through a small window, Beverly could see the cadet upperclassman in charge of the room locking up his computer desk. As they waited for the cadet to leave, Dewley gave them a lecture on the components of the computer system.

Beverly wasn't really listening to Dewley and took the time to look around at the computers in the study room. Several times in the past, she visited the building with Dewley, who bragged that the Academy was lucky—their computers ranked with those at Starfleet Command headquarters. She was always amazed at the intricate layers of crystal memory cards and relays. Lights flashed on and off on the machines, and rows of computer monitors blinked with data and messages. The study room always seemed to be a busy place, yet it was usually eerily silent. For some reason, she thought all computers were always beeping and humming—maybe because of the noisy, outdated computers they used on Arvada III. The quiet computers in the study room showed her that the machines had come a long way. The scientists on

Arvada would have loved to replace their archaic machines with those from Starfleet.

When she finally listened again, Dewley was lecturing about computer codes. After about five minutes, Beverly sighed with relief as the main computer room door hissed open and the upperclassman left for lunch. He nodded to Dewley as he left, and Dewley continued his "lecture."

As the cadet disappeared around the corner, Imto grabbed the data padds from the others. He quickly took up his station at the door, ready to signal if someone headed in his direction. Dewley quietly motioned to Beverly and Claire to follow. As they watched, he punched several templates on the computer panel to open the door. The door stayed closed. Dewley frowned, then pushed another combination on the panel. A second later, the door hissed open. He smiled as he waved them into the main computer room.

No one spoke a word. The room was smaller than Beverly had imagined. As she looked around, Beverly understood why Dewley mentioned it would be useless to try to hide if they were caught. Rows of computer consoles filled the room. And along one wall were neat stacks of computer tapes.

In a few quick, short steps, Claire was standing next to the tape stacks. "Thank goodness Wiley keeps such good records," she whispered. Beverly and Dewley quickly shushed her. She shrugged as she continued to search the first three stacks. Each tape disk was neatly arranged according to month and day—and in less than a minute, she found a tape with the correct date.

Grabbing the purplish disk from the stack, Claire

reached over and handed the tape to Beverly. Quickly slipping it into the computer console next to Dewley, Beverly stepped back. Dewley's hands danced across the console panel and a computer screen began to roll through line after line of data. Beverly's eyes darted back and forth as she checked the passing data on the screen. "There," she said suddenly in a low voice. She pointed to a line of text and numbers on the screen, "That's it. 'Benthos asteroid belt' and 'Romulan Bird-of-Prey,' simulations number six and seven."

Dewley pulled another computer tape from his jumpsuit pocket. Pushing his tape into the console, he hit several more panels and smiled. "Copy complete," he whispered. Beverly pulled out the original tape and started to hand it back to Claire.

They all froze as three short whistles reached their ears. "It's Imto's signal," Dewley whispered urgently. Beverly had a sinking feeling in her stomach. Someone was coming.

Beverly pushed the tape into Claire's hand and turned to see Dewley scramble toward the front door. Suddenly, she heard Claire yelp.

"I dropped it!"

Claire was on her knees, trying to reach between two computer stacks for the purplish tape. She groaned as she strained to reach the disk. "My—arm's—too—short!"

"Here," whispered Beverly anxiously. She bent down near Claire. "Let me get it. My arm is longer." Beverly reached between the stacks, just barely grasping the tape. As she pulled, it wedged itself deeper between the two stacks. As she twisted it to the right and pulled hard, the tape suddenly popped out of its trap. She stood up with the tape in her hand and quickly put it into its proper place. Claire grabbed Beverly's arm and pulled her roommate toward the door.

But it was too late. "Hey, you two! What are you doing in here? This is an authorized area!" came a loud voice from across the room. They froze and looked over to see the cadet upperclassman standing in the doorway, his hands on his hips.

"So much for long lunches," Claire muttered under her breath and leaned against a computer console. Beverly looked at her roommate and grimaced.

Beverly knew Dewley and Imto had made it out of the building—but she and Claire had been caught.

Admiral Muti stood beside Commander Wiley. They both stared at Beverly and Claire as the senior cadet escorted them into the admiral's office.

Wiley did not wait for Muti to speak. "I want them out of the Academy," he said, glaring at the cadets.

Muti turned and frowned at Wiley. "Apparently, you have forgotten something, Commander. You, too, are being investigated at this time. Please," she said, indicating the door. "I would like to talk to the cadets alone."

Wiley briskly walked across the room. As the door hissed closed behind him, the admiral walked forward and stood in front of Beverly and Claire. "I don't have to tell you—you're both in deep trouble," she began. "As cadets, you have access to the computer center, and with clearance, the main computer room. But you broke into Starfleet property without clearance—and that is a serious offense. Commander Wiley said that nothing was missing, but apparently a simulation tape was copied. Is that correct?''

"Yes, sir," answered Beverly.

"Do you want to tell me about it?"

"We were checking on a simulation," Claire responded. Her voice was shaking.

"The one in which Cadet Peterson was hurt?" she asked. Claire nodded. "Don't you think Starfleet can carry out its own investigation?" The cadets did not answer. "I know there were others involved, too. What are their names?"

"Sir, I take full responsibility—it was all my idea—" Beverly started.

"And mine, too," interrupted Claire.

Muti stared at the cadets for a few seconds. "This matter will be further investigated. And we will find out who helped you. But for right now, I must put you both on probation. I did warn you," she added, reaching back on her desk. She touched the screen of her computer. "There will be no leave for either of you, and you are not allowed to leave campus," she recited. "In addition, any further violation of the rules will mean immediate expulsion."

She turned back to the cadets. She seemed to hesitate before she spoke. "Off the record, cadets, I shuddered when I saw your names on report again. Both of you have been a great disappointment to me. I bent over backward to give you another chance," she said, frowning. "Don't you realize that not only are you letting Starfleet down, but you're letting yourselves down? Just think of how hard you worked to get here. Please, for your own sakes, stay out of trouble until we can clear up this mess. Cadets dismissed."

Beverly and Claire left Muti's office and walked slowly back toward the dorm. Even the walk through campus didn't cheer Beverly up.

Now she was *really* in trouble. How could she tell her grandmother about being on probation? She pictured her grandmother's face as she received the message. Probably the same disappointed look as when Beverly accidentally pulled out all her grandmother's only heirloom Scottish thistle from the garden six years ago.

No, this was worse—and it could get much worse. What if she was kicked out of the Academy? All the time her grandmother had spent teaching Beverly and all the high hopes she had for her granddaughter would be crushed with a single message from the Academy. And if she were kicked out of the Academy—especially for getting into trouble—what other medical school would want her? *There is only one thing to do: find out how and why Peter Peterson—and I—were shocked during the simulation. Then the only time I'll have to leave the Academy is if I choose to leave.*

They turned as a voice called from behind. "Bev! Claire! What happened? We made it out, but we never saw you again," inquired Dewley, catching up with them.

"We got caught," explained Beverly. "We just came back from Muti's and we're really in trouble now. She put us on probation."

Dewley whistled. "Gee, I'm sorry. It's sort of like Max Wiley."

"Max Wiley?" Beverly said, puzzled.

"Rumor has it he's under investigation until the Peter

Peterson case is solved," Dewley answered. "I heard he can't teach until this shock incident is cleared up. And it probably didn't help that we broke into the computer center and copied the tape."

Beverly blinked. She didn't realize that by breaking into the computer center, she would get Max Wiley into further trouble. In fact, she really didn't think *she* would be in so much trouble.

"Dewley—what happened to the tape?" she asked.

Dewley smiled and slipped a white computer tape out of his jumpsuit pocket. "I was able to get some time on Holodeck Three."

"You ran it? Was anyone hurt?"

"No. I grabbed Imto, Gren, T'Kavar, and we played the copied Benthos asteroid and Romulan Bird-of-Prey sections over and over again," he said, his usual smile disappearing for a moment. "We each played a part in the simulations—and even with eight eyes, we couldn't find anything suspicious. We even tried scanning with your and Claire's holodeck medical tricorders. No one was shocked. They worked fine. All the other tricorders worked fine. Everything worked fine."

Beverly looked puzzled. "What? I thought for sure it would show *something*. Now what do we do? And—"

As Dewley passed the tape to Beverly, it fell to the ground. A passing brown-haired cadet grabbed the tape and handed it back to Dewley.

"Hey, Crusher," said Dewley, grinning at the upper-classman. "Thanks, Jack."

"Sure, Dewley, see you in class."

Beverly smiled at the upperclassman as she took the recovered tape from Dewley.

79

"And what, Bev?"

"Umm . . . I think I have an idea," she said, shaking her head and turning back to her two friends. "We've been banging our heads against a wall so far. But I think there *is* someone who can help us. Someone who knows everything about computers. Have you two ever heard of a cadet named Data?"

CHAPTER

9

Everyone at Starfleet Academy knew about Cadet Data.
Since arriving at the Academy a year ago, his reputation
as an expert on computers—or almost anything else, for
that matter—was well-known. Data was an android who
was found on Omicron Theta four years ago by the crew
of the Federation starship *Tripoli*. He was the only re-
maining being at the colony. The four hundred and eleven
colonists had entered all their memories into Data—and
all had died when a crystal entity attacked the planet.

After several weeks onboard the *Tripoli*, Data decided
to enter Starfleet Academy. It seemed like the right thing
to do. After all, Starfleet Academy was the perfect place
for Data to grow and understand the universe around
him. The Academy offered a cadet the chance to learn,
explore—and especially to confront and experience the
unknown.

But it wasn't easy for Data to enter Starfleet Academy. Before he could enter the Academy as a cadet, he had to wait for Starfleet to make an important decision: Was Data a sentient lifeform?

To find out, Starfleet put Data through test after test. They poked him and prodded him. They gave him tests to determine his ability to think and reason. They asked him question after question. And in the end—three years later, thanks to Starfleet bureaucracy—Data was allowed to enter the Academy as a first-year cadet. The officials at Starfleet had decided Data was indeed sentient.

Beverly found Cadet Data's quarters and pushed the chime at the door. In response, the door swooshed open, revealing a room with few decorations. "Cadet Data?" she asked, looking around the door and into the room.

"I am here. Please come in," said a pleasant voice from behind a computer console in the corner.

She had never seen Data before. She imagined, like many people who had never met him, that the android would be stiff and less animated. But she found Data was different. His fingers moved smoothly over the computer console. And his eyes moved quickly back and forth as he read the computer screen in front of him.

Data's form was human, but with several differences: His eyes were yellow, his skin was a pale gold color, and his dark hair was slicked back. Someone once told her that Data had the strength of five humans and could move faster than most humans. She also heard that Data's positronic brain was amazing—it processed information as fast as a fair-sized computer.

As she approached the computer where Data sat, he

stood up and extended his hand. "I am Cadet Data. Can I help you?"

Beverly took his cool hand in hers and shook it. "Cadet Beverly Howard. I'm in Starfleet Medical. First year."

"Then you arrived three point seven weeks ago with the rest of the new cadets?"

"Yes," she said, with a laugh, "but I never figured it out to the nearest tenth."

Data did not laugh, but stared at her. "Can I help you with something?" he asked in his soft voice.

Beverly wanted to ask him so many questions: What did he eat, did his hair grow, did he know how to sing, did he have a pulse, or what would happen if he scratched his hand—or even if he could scratch his hand. She wanted to know what he was studying, if he would ever want to go into medicine, or if he liked to watch a sunset. But she held back the many questions and concentrated on her mission. Maybe one day, she would have a long talk with Data.

"Cadet Data—"

"Please call me Data."

"Thank you. And please call me Beverly," she responded. "Data, I hear that you are an expert in computers—hardware and programming. May I ask you some questions about computers? It's for a class I'm taking."

Data cocked his head to the side in a very human gesture. She wondered if the movement was programmed or if he picked up the habit by watching people around him. "Why do you not ask your professor?"

"He's very busy right now. Plus, I thought you could give me a different viewpoint."

1995

Data moved from the computer console and offered Beverly a nearby chair. He sat in the chair next to her, his back very straight. Beverly thought it looked uncomfortable, but he seemed to be at ease. "Most of my questions deal with holodeck simulations," she said, folding her hands on her lap. "I'm taking the Medical Emergencies course—"

"The course for first-year medical cadets," Data interrupted.

"Yes," she continued. "I really like the course but I'm wondering about the programming of a simulation. I wondered if it's possible to modify a holodeck simulation."

"Yes, it is possible," said the android. "A person familiar with holodeck simulation programming can make small modifications, such as changing an evergreen tree to an oak tree. Or they can make larger changes, such as changing a desert to an ocean. It is relatively easy. You see, a holographic environment simulator produces an image with the holographic imagery subsection, responsible for the realistic backgrounds seen in the simulation. The solid characters and objects are composed of solid matter arranged by a transporter-based replicator. Each one of these is related to the omni-directional holo diode, which projects the forcefields—"

"Data . . . good," interrupted Beverly. She held up a hand, realizing that Data could probably go on forever explaining the intricacies of the holodeck. "That's excellent. So it *is* possible to modify a simulation."

"Yes."

"If you ran the simulation again, would you be able to detect the change?"

"Yes," he said, his gold eyes staring at her intently. "If you changed the holographic element, it would be possible to detect when the program was run again. That is, if you as a sentient being viewed the universe in the visible part of the spectrum you would notice the difference. As you probably know, holo-images are only created to be seen in the visible range of the electromagnetic spectrum, no doubt, to—"

"Yes, Data, thank you. But what if it were a subtle change, would you still notice the modification?"

"You would have to know what you are looking for—especially if it were a small change. Perhaps I could detect such a change, as I have found my senses are usually keener than the senses of a human. But you, Beverly, might not be able to detect such small changes."

"So it is possible to modify a simulation without noticing," she said, almost to herself, sorting out Data's words, "almost like programming a robot to . . . oh," she stammered, her face flushing. "I mean . . . I'm sorry—"

"Beverly. Do not worry. Your comment does not offend me. More accurately, I am an android. I do not have feelings such as anger or embarrassment. It is not in my programming." Beverly smiled at Data. She wished, too, she didn't have to feel embarrassed at the moment, but then realized she preferred to have emotions. She wondered if Data wished he could have emotions. "I might add that even though you could not detect the modification of the program," he continued as if nothing had happened, "the record of such a change would be imprinted on the computer tape."

"Could a computer detect the change?"

"Yes. A computer could detect such a change. But,

Beverly, as you must know, it is against Starfleet rules to modify a tape for a cadet simulation class."

As if that would stop someone from actually doing it, Beverly thought. "Unless you had the correct authorization," she added out loud.

"That is true. Beverly," he said suddenly, leaning in her direction, "now may I ask you a question?"

She looked at Data and nodded.

"Are you contemplating doing something illegal with a holodeck simulation?"

"No, Data. Not at all." Beverly sighed and made a face.

"Are you in pain, Beverly? Do you need medical assistance?"

"No," she said, moving uncomfortably in her seat.

Data's voice was almost a whisper. "Is something wrong?"

"Oh, Data," she said, standing up and walking over to a nearby computer console. "One of my friends—my roommate, as a matter of fact—is in trouble. And I really want to help her. But I can't seem to figure out what happened."

Data tilted his head again. "Perhaps I can be of assistance. Based on your questions, I assume your roommate was involved in the Medical Emergencies class in which Cadet Peter Peterson was injured. And I assume also that she was directly involved in the injury, perhaps in the same simulation as Cadet Peterson when he was hurt."

Beverly nodded. "You'd make a great detective, Data."

"On the contrary. I am a Starfleet Academy cadet

training to be an officer. As you know, we are all trained to reason, to ask questions, and to find solutions. And we are all here to help each other."

Beverly sat down again and smiled. Maybe she *did* fit into the Academy—after all, she had been doing such reasoning, too. With enthusiasm, she proceeded to tell Data what she had found so far: How preliminary studies showed it was not the holodeck. How several of her friends had checked the simulation tape and found nothing. And how Commander Wiley had dismissed her shock from the holodeck's medical tricorder.

Data hesitated for a moment, almost as if he was absorbing Beverly's words. "I assume your roommate does not have the expertise to modify a simulation." Beverly nodded. "And no doubt Commander Wiley was in the holodeck at the time. He is known to be one of the best simulations experts in Starfleet. He would have the ability and the opportunity to change a simulation—and he could have made the change quickly."

"But, Data, why create a shock that would knock the socks off a cadet?"

"Perhaps you should ask the commander," he said, then hesitated. His face was as straight as when they started the conversation. "But, Beverly, I do not think such a possibility exists. Although there have been reports from the twentieth century in which people struck by cloud-to-ground lightning did, literally, have their 'socks knocked off,' as you say. But I find that such an allegory is usually incomplete in its accuracy. I believe it is called a legend or folktale."

Beverly laughed. Data's face looked slightly confused as she stood up and held out her hand. "It's just a figure of speech, Data. But you're definitely right. It's time to confront Commander Wiley again. And this time, if it's possible, I want Admiral Muti to be there."

"I hope I have helped."

"Data, you have helped me more than you'll ever know."

As the door of her quarters whooshed open, Beverly was surrounded by the smell of fresh lemons. Claire was at her desk, a steaming mug of herbal tea in her hand. "That smells wonderful," said Beverly. She collapsed on her bed and closed her eyes.

"Was Cadet Data overwhelming?" Claire asked, sipping her tea.

"No," Beverly said, turning over and facing her roommate. "He was wonderful, intelligent—and he agrees you had nothing to do with the simulation problem."

Claire jumped up from her chair, enthusiastically yelling, "Yes!"

"If you're going to yell," interrupted Beverly, rubbing her temples, "please get me some lemon tea."

"No problem." As Claire ordered the tea from the replicator, Beverly told her what Data said. "It is possible to make subtle changes to the simulation," explained Beverly, "but only by someone who had authorization. Data and I both agreed—it's time to face Wiley again. And this time, I think Admiral Muti should be there."

Before Claire could reply, a communication chime sounded. Beverly reached for her comm padd. "Ah, Beverly," came the familiar voice. "How is your investigation proceeding?"

"Hi, Mrs. Oner. Fine, I think," she replied. She motioned to Claire to come over to the comm padd, then turned back to the Muldanian woman on the view screen. "I just got back from talking to Cadet Data."

"Yes, I know him. He has visited my restaurant several times. I find he is shy." Beverly saw Mrs. Oner's blue eyes twinkle with the memory of Data. "I also know he is very good at computers. Did he help you?"

Beverly nodded and related her conversation with Data. After she was finished, Mrs. Oner tilted her head. "I will go with you to Admiral Muti's—she is a friend of mine."

"You know the admiral?" asked Claire, looking at the comm padd screen from over Beverly's shoulder.

Mrs. Oner nodded. "She is a regular at my café. A very interesting woman."

"She also put us on probation," added Claire.

"Yes, I know. I will meet you at the admiral's office, in about one quarter hour. Is that all right with you?" They nodded and cut off the comm pad link.

Beverly and Claire walked as fast as possible through campus to Admiral Muti's office. They didn't have long to wait for Mrs. Oner. The Muldanian woman arrived shortly after the cadets—complete with the usual smile on her face. She was dressed in white, with a light yellow shawl covering her shoulders. She also carried a small wicker basket in her right hand.

As the senior cadet led them into the room, Beverly thought of how she had seen enough of the admiral's office in the past few days. Admiral Muti had a quizzical look on her face as she saw Beverly and Claire. She smiled when she saw Mrs. Oner.

"Mrs. Oner," gushed Muti. She extended both her hands to the older woman. "How are you?"

Mrs. Oner squeezed Muti's hands in her left hand. "Ah, Miomi. I bring you a gift." She handed the small basket to the admiral and watched.

Muti opened the basket and sniffed. "Beeswitsh! I haven't had beeswitsh since I left my sister's house in Old Kenya. Now I'm really curious why you're here," exclaimed the admiral. Beverly thought the admiral seemed a little nervous around the Muldanian.

"Ah, yes. I bring my two good friends with me," Mrs. Oner said. She turned slightly toward Beverly and Claire.

"Yes, we have met before," said Muti, her face turning stern, "in fact, too many times, Ambassador."

The two cadets looked quizzically at each other, then turned to Mrs. Oner. "Ambassador?" they asked in unison.

Muti smiled again and looked at Mrs. Oner. "It's not something that is well known. Mrs. Oner is friends with most higher officials at Starfleet Command, and is one of the most respected ambassadors from her world."

The Muldanian turned to Claire and took her hand. "Ah, Claire. My people believe that their ambassadors should meet all types of beings from all cultures on an equal basis. On Earth, as in many other cultures, it is the meal where people are most relaxed. That is why I run the café. And it would not be right to call myself 'Ambassador' in front of my guests, correct? There, I am 'Mrs. Oner,' even though I am still ambassador for my people."

Claire stammered. "Then . . . then 'Mrs. Oner'—"

"Is not my real name," she finished. "You could not

pronounce my real name. It includes sounds that most humans cannot imitate. Now, Beverly," she continued, turning to the cadet and bowing slightly, "please tell Miomi Muti your story."

Beverly smiled at the reference to Muti's first name while the admiral cleared her throat in an authoritative manner. Beverly told the story of how she obtained and checked a copy of the tape for any tampering—and found no evidence. She also mentioned the conversation with Cadet Data and her theories on what happened to the simulation. "I think someone made a subtle, unnoticeable change to the computer program. Claire is not a programmer, so I don't believe she caused Peter to get hurt. Not only that, a person needs authorization to modify the computer program."

"So that leaves Commander Wiley?" Muti asked, frowning.

Beverly hesitated, then looked into the admiral's dark eyes. "Commander Wiley did have the correct authorization. But I don't think someone with the commander's background and enthusiasm for his students and the Academy would jeopardize his chances of staying in Starfleet. I really don't think the commander would tamper with the simulation . . . sir."

Muti sighed and turned to her computer console. "Computer, where is Commander Max Wiley?"

"Commander Max Wiley is in Holodeck Four."

"The Medical Emergencies class holodeck," she said softly. "Cadet Terry. Cancel all my communications for the next hour. I'll be in Holodeck Four." The admiral picked up a data padd and briskly announced, "Cadets? It's time we faced the commander and his holodeck simulation. And Ambassador—we could use your help, too."

As they walked to Holodeck Four, cadets passing the group acknowledged Admiral Muti with a curt salute. Beverly chuckled to herself as she realized how it must have piqued the cadets' curiosity: Why would two first-year cadets be walking with the Commanding Officer of Starfleet Medical—and Mrs. Oner?

Just before they reached the building, a voice called out from behind the group. Beverly stopped and turned to see a cadet quickly walking toward her, a padd in his hand.

Cadet Data stopped before her. "May I talk with you, Beverly?"

CHAPTER

10

Data nodded to the group standing on the walkway. "Admiral Muti. Mrs. Oner. And—"

"Claire . . . Cadet Claire Voy," said the cadet, staring intently at Data. Beverly knew why Claire was staring—she had never met the android. She wondered if it bothered Data that everyone stared at him. Then again, he did tell her he didn't have such emotions.

"And Cadet Voy. Beverly," he continued, turning back to her, "I have some additional news for you."

"Cadet Data. Does this concern a holodeck simulation?" asked Muti, stepping closer to the android.

"Yes, sir," he responded, nodding to the admiral. "Earlier in the₁day, I talked with Cadet Howard about a holodeck simulation. A holographic environment simulator produces an image with the holographic imagery subsection, responsible for the realistic backgrounds seen in the simulation. The solid characters and objects are composed of—"

"Cadet Data," interrupted the admiral. "We don't really need a lecture on holographic simulations."

"Yes, sir. As I said, I explained to Cadet Howard that someone familiar with holodeck simulation programming could easily change a holodeck program. But I have some new information for Cadet Howard—there is another way to 'fix' a simulation. I do not know why I did not think of it before. Perhaps it was because I was working on the pressure analysis of a warp field core in a—"

"Cadet!" the admiral interrupted again. "Your idea on fixing the simulation? Please?"

"Yes, sir," he said, a slight frown forming on his face. "There is another way to modify a holodeck simulation—without actually detecting it. It is possible to enter what is called a computer virus into a computer system. There are many types of viruses, including those that—once they accomplish their tasks—can be removed from the computer."

Claire frowned. "Removed?"

The android nodded. "A virus-type program can be entered into a computer via a computer disk. The virus that is sent into a simulation could cause part of the holodeck simulation to act differently. For example, a virus could cause a computer console to produce incorrect information, such as an incorrect warp speed reading at the helm. When the program had done its work, the virus could be 'called back' to its home—or to the awaiting computer disk—without leaving a visible trace on the simulation tape. The helm would then report the simulation's correct warp speed. The computer disk could then be removed from the computer console. No one, except the person who entered and called back the virus, would know. It is possible."

"What about the fail-safes?" asked Beverly.

"The virus program could essentially overwhelm the simulation program and cause the fail-safes not to work," he explained. "Or the actual virus-type program may include an additional override program that would cancel the fail-safes. But one would have to have the correct security codes to override the fail-safes."

No one said a word.

"Perhaps this type of computer virus can be best explained with an analogy," he continued. "A fine example is the nineteenth century Sherlock Holmes detective story, 'The Speckled Band,' by Sir Arthur Conan Doyle. In this mystery story, a woman is killed for an unknown reason. Holmes eventually determines that a swamp adder, a deadly snake, slipped into the victim's room through a vent, bit the helpless girl, then glided back to the killer waiting in another room. The woman was killed seemingly without a trace of who or what killed her. Although a computer virus does not bite."

"I think we know that, Cadet," said Muti.

"Yes, sir."

"But if it doesn't leave a trace, how can we find out if it's true?" Beverly asked.

"As I said," Data continued, "it leaves no visible trace that can be detected in the simulation tape. But it will leave a data trace in the program."

The admiral suddenly smiled at Data. "Thank you, Cadet. You have been very helpful. Perhaps you'd like to accompany us to Holodeck Four. I think your explanations will greatly enhance this investigation."

"I would be glad to help, Admiral Muti."

Muti turned on her heel and walked toward the holodeck building, the others following close behind.

Holodeck Four's door swished open in response to Admiral Muti's commands. She entered the holodeck first, followed by Mrs. Oner and the three cadets. Wiley was standing on a chair behind a computer, trying to reach a computer tape on top of a tall console. A puzzled frown formed on his face as he stepped off the chair, one arm filled with computer tapes. "Oh, Admiral Muti. Hello, sir," he said, looking puzzled at the admiral. "What's wrong?"

"Commander Wiley, I hope you have a few minutes," she said. She stood in front of the console and clasped her hands behind her. "We have several questions and concerns we would like to discuss with you."

"We? Mrs. Oner, Cadet Data—what are you doing here? And why are these cadets here?" he demanded, his face turning red. He juggled the tapes in both hands.

"I asked them here, Commander," responded Muti. "They're making their own inquiries about the Peterson simulation. Mrs. Oner and Cadet Data have been assisting the cadets. And I'm interested in hearing your responses to all of their questions."

"With all due respect, Admiral Muti, I thought the guilty party in this case was decided. This cadet," he said, nodding at Claire, "probably caused the problem. I still don't know what she touched or how she did it, but I'm working on it." Claire straightened and glared

97

at Wiley. Beverly grabbed her arm, holding her back from any response.

Beverly could feel her legs shaking as she walked forward. She felt more nervous than when she played the lead in a musical on Caldos IV. "Admiral?"

"By all means, Cadet Howard. Please relate your story to the commander."

Beverly stated her theories about the computer simulation. She mentioned how easy it was to modify a tape, how easy it was to change an existing tape in subtle ways, and override fail-safes as long as one had the correct authorization.

"Now Cadet Data," Muti said, turning to Data, "Please to explain to Commander Wiley what you and Cadet Howard were discussing earlier. Wasn't it something about a possible type of virus within the computer simulation?"

"What? A virus? Don't be ridiculous," Wiley scoffed, dropping the stack of disks haphazardly on the computer console. "We have programs that eliminate viruses within a computer program."

"True," responded Data, unflappable. "But it is possible if you were an expert at programming computer simulations to enter a type of virus within a program, then extract the virus."

Wiley sputtered and turned to Muti. "Are you accusing me of tampering with my own simulations with a virus to . . . to harm others—especially one of my cadets?"

The admiral walked behind the console and faced the commander. "I am suggesting that we get to the bottom of this mystery," she answered. "And the only way to find out is to face the physical evidence. Commander, I suggest you check out the simulation in question."

The holodeck door suddenly hissed open and Cadet Stephen Cody entered the room, carrying several computer simulation tapes. He hesitated as he stared at the group, then walked over to a computer console. He turned and began to sort the tapes.

"Cadet Cody," said Wiley in a stern voice. "Get me the tape from the day Cadet Peter Peterson was hurt. It's in the stack of tapes I brought over from the computer center today—over there on the desk." Stephen stopped and did not move. "Cadet Cody, I gave you an order. Get the tape."

Stephen shifted uncomfortably. "Sir, I . . . I don't—"

"I'll get it myself," Wiley grumbled, pushing past Stephen and looking through the tapes on the desk. After a few seconds, he pulled out a purplish tape. "Sir," he said, reaching over and handing the disk to the admiral.

"After you, Commander Wiley, please," said Muti, indicating the computer console.

Wiley stepped up to the console and pushed the tape into a slot. He pushed several panels, then spoke: "Computer."

"Working."

"Please analyze the tape and answer the following questions. Does the tape contain the simulation from the Medical Emergencies class from—" He hesitated.

"Twenty-nine point three hours ago, sir," Data interjected.

"Thank you, Cadet." Wiley nodded to Data. "Computer, the class from twenty-nine point three hours ago."

"Affirmative."

"Analyze the simulation of the starship *U.S.S. Gallant* under attack by a Romulan Bird-of-Prey," he ordered, then looked at Beverly, "and the simulation of the shuttlecraft traveling to Pella through an asteroid belt."

"Working."

"Are the simulations correct?"

Beverly held her breath as the computer answered.

"Affirmative."

Wiley smiled at the admiral, and bowed slightly to Mrs. Oner. "My investigation shows the same thing. The tape is fine. The simulations are fine."

"I believe Data has questions," Mrs. Oner said softly.

Data nodded. He stepped in front of Wiley and then turned to Admiral Muti. "Admiral Muti," he asked, "With your permission?"

"Of course, Cadet Data. Be my guest."

"Computer. Are there any anomalies in the simulations?"

"Negative."

Wiley smiled again. Data thought for a moment. "Computer. Does the tape show any residual signatures that differ from the original program?"

"Working. Affirmative. A secondary program has entered and exited the program. Residual data was found in sectors three, eighteen, and ninety-four. There is no damage to the simulations."

Data turned to the admiral. "A secondary program would be a virus-type program. You see, Admiral Muti," he explained, "no matter what type of virus is sent through the system, there will always be traces left— pieces of computer code, if you will, remain."

"Yes," said Beverly, turning to Muti. "The human

Loyalties

body is the same way with some viruses. We have anti-
bodies that resist certain viruses in our body, so we ap-
pear to be healthy. But there is always a trace of the
virus left within us. Like the chicken pox virus—it's always in a person after they've had the disease, but anti-
bodies keep it at bay most of the time."

"An interesting comparison, Cadet Howard," responded Data. "Not completely inaccurate."

For a moment, no one spoke or moved.

Beverly looked around at the group.

A *virus* . . .

CHAPTER

11

"That's it," Beverly whispered to no one in particular. "Admiral, I remember now where I've heard someone talking about viruses before. It was in class. Medical Ethics," she said and turned to the cadet across the room. "It was Stephen Cody—Commander Wiley's assistant."

She looked over at Mrs. Oner and saw the older woman nod. Beverly was shocked to see her face neutral, the usual smile on her face gone.

Wiley was stunned. He slowly turned to Stephen, his mouth open in amazement.

Stephen looked around like a caged animal. "Don't be silly. I—"

Beverly pointed at Stephen. "You were the one who said you wanted to work on getting viruses out of computers. You said you had been doing it for years. And

I assume if you can get them out, you can certainly get them in."

Suddenly, Cody ran past Wiley and a computer console, heading for the door. Before Beverly realized it, he was running in her direction. Her reflexes were quick—and he fell to the floor as she stuck out a long leg in front of him.

Data was suddenly by her side, pulling Stephen to his feet. The cadet struggled for a moment, then stopped. "Let go of me," Stephen growled, shrugging off Data's grasp. "I . . . I'll stay."

Wiley moved forward to face Stephen. "Stephen," he said quietly, tilting his head to one side. "Why?"

"What do you mean 'why'?" he responded, his face contorting with anger. He looked at Admiral Muti. "I really didn't want to hurt anyone," he said to her, then turned to Wiley. "I just wanted to get *you* in trouble—and hopefully kicked out of Starfleet."

"Me? You wanted to get *me* kicked out of Starfleet?" Wiley asked.

"Yeah, you," he answered. He looked directly into Wiley's eyes. "Everyone in my family has been in Starfleet. My grandfather, my father and mother, my aunts and uncles. And my sister wanted to get into Starfleet Medical more than anything else in the world. For years, I listened to her talking about Starfleet Medical—about being a doctor. She wanted to help other cultures, to become a doctor on a Starfleet starship," he said. He shook his head with the memory. "But she didn't get in. And she missed entering the program because of just one person—Commander Max Wiley."

Stephen leaned on a nearby desk, his back toward

Muti and the others. "Beverly was right," he continued. "I entered a type of computer virus into the simulation. As the commander's assistant, I knew his entire schedule—and after a while, I was even able to work out his computer authorization code. I've worked on computer viruses for years. Since I know how to get them out of a program, I know how to get them in. So I slipped my customized virus program into the computer earlier in the day. I even kept up a fight with Imto Partigle so I would come to class late—just to add to the confusion and throw off suspicion."

Without saying a word to interrupt Stephen, Beverly nodded to the admiral, confirming that Stephen had come to class late.

"It was easy for me to send the virus through the program at any time," he continued. "I just had to push a few panels at my console. The virus program was sent out to seek a holodeck medical tricorder. When it eventually found one, the program would cause the scanner to send out a signal—an asynchronous invisible field that shocks the scanned person. I tried sending it out during Beverly's simulation, but she was pointing the medical tricorder at a holodeck-simulated Andorian ensign. So all that happened was that small shock she felt—not enough to cause suspicion. I called back the virus—and that's when I decided to send it out during the Romulan Bird-of-Prey simulation."

Beverly listened as he further explained how he didn't know who would be the team for the simulation, but it didn't matter. She shivered as she realized she could have been badly hurt—or could have been chosen for the fated simulation. She watched Claire's face turn pale as Stephen continued his explanation.

"I never tried the program on anyone so I didn't know what would happen. But I didn't really mean to hurt anyone—I thought the dosage would be like a light stun with a phaser. I didn't know Peter would get hurt.

"During the confusion after Peter was hurt, I called the virus back into my personal computer tape so no one would find it. After everyone left, I stayed behind to make sure that any question asked during an inquiry would show the simulation had not been tampered with—at least I thought I did," he said, pointing to Data. "I hadn't counted on Data showing up to ask questions."

"I did not 'show up,' as you say," declared Data. "It was Cadet Howard who brought up the possibility. I reasoned out the actualities."

As Data motioned to Beverly, Stephen turned to her and shook his head. "I should have known that a future Starfleet space doctor would be the one who kept asking questions. Why couldn't you just leave well enough alone?"

"I was trying to help . . . some friends," Beverly said softly.

Stephen ignored her and turned back to face Wiley. "And at the bottom of all this," emphasized the cadet, "was you. I knew the accidents would eventually be your fault. After all, the professor in charge must make sure everything is correctly maintained for the cadet simulations."

Wiley ran his hand through his short hair. "Stephen," he said, almost in a whisper. "Your sister was just not right for Starfleet this year. It happens. We feel there are some students who are not quite ready for Starfleet. Your sister did poorly in the simulation entrance exam I gave her—that's why I didn't recommend her entry into Starfleet at this time."

"Yes, but the simulation wasn't fair," Stephen retorted. "She was thrown into a shuttlecraft that was adrift—how would she know how to start the shuttle once it shut down?"

"We weren't asking her to start up the shuttle," Wiley said. "We were trying to see her reaction to an emergency situation. Even if she didn't know what to do, there were certain responses we were looking for. But we . . . I felt that she did not act appropriately for a first-year cadet. That's all. And Stephen, she can try again next year."

Stephen smirked at the commander. "That's what she's going to do—and if you were out of the picture, I know she would have a better chance. That's why I did it," he said. He flopped down into a nearby chair, as if he was too exhausted to stand.

Admiral Muti frowned as she stood in front of Stephen's chair. She looked down at him, then turned to Wiley and the three cadets. "Commander, you and the cadets are dismissed."

Beverly looked back as the door hissed closed. She saw Stephen put his head in his hands. Mrs. Oner was standing next to Admiral Muti. "Your sister may or may not get into Starfleet Academy next year," the admiral was saying, "but if she does, she'll be here without you."

The three cadets walked in silence out of the holodeck building, the commander following close behind. Beverly was glad they had finally found out the truth—for both Claire's and Commander Wiley's sakes—but she was sad that Stephen Cody was guilty. She knew he had thrown away his chance of ever becoming a Starfleet officer.

Beverly took a deep breath as they reached the outside. The warm breeze off the ocean seemed to refresh her.

"I will be going back to my quarters now, Beverly," said Data, turning to face her. "I am pleased everything has been resolved."

"So am I, Data," she answered. She took Data's hand and gave it a quick squeeze. He tilted his head, and for a moment Beverly thought his face registered surprise. Apparently, he was not used to such a friendly handshake. "Thanks so much for your help, Data. I couldn't have done it without you."

The android nodded briefly to her. "If I may say so: you, too, Beverly, would make an excellent detective. You have the commitment to find out difficult answers. I have also noticed that such a quality is the sign of an excellent doctor—and Starfleet officer."

Beverly smiled at him and straightened her shoulders. "Thank you, Cadet Data. I hope we meet again."

He turned and nodded to Claire and Commander Wiley, then walked away.

"I owe you both an apology," came Wiley's voice from behind the cadets. "Cadet Howard, I didn't believe that you had been shocked. And Cadet Voy, I really thought you did something wrong during the simulation. I had no idea it was my own assistant who caused the problem. I believe I was blinded by my own troubles."

Claire smiled at the commander and held out her

hand. "I'm just glad we could get to the bottom of this," she said, shaking Wiley's offered hand. Beverly reached out and also shook the commander's hand.

He hesitated for a moment. "May I ask why you both were so diligently looking for who was guilty?"

Beverly smiled, relieved to tell the truth. "I knew Claire wasn't guilty—and I really didn't believe you were guilty. I know how much you love Starfleet. I learned that from attending your classes. Deep down inside, I just couldn't believe that you would ever jeopardize your chances of staying here." *And if anything rubs off on me, I hope it's the same type of commitment to what I do,* she thought.

It was the first time Beverly had ever seen Wiley smile. She liked the effect, and hoped she would see it more often. "Thank you, Cadet Howard," he answered. "I really do love being in Starfleet. But Stephen Cody did, too."

"But I think he loved his sister's dream of being a doctor more," she responded.

It was early evening when Admiral Muti called Beverly and Claire to her office. Wiley was there, too—standing tall and smiling broadly.

". . . And I have these two cadets to thank, along with Cadet Data," Wiley was saying. "Admiral, I hereby personally withdraw all complaints against these two cadets."

"Consider it done," answered Muti. "Commander, the investigation is over. You may return to your normal duties. And now you have your work cut out for you—finding someone to replace Cadet Cody."

Wiley's face dropped for a moment, then he smiled. "I know just the person—or persons," he said, turning to the cadets. "Cadets Howard and Voy, I am very impressed with your thoroughness and ability to reason. I am requesting that you both become my new assistants for holodeck simulations. I could use two excellent cadets like you." Wiley turned back to Muti. "Now I realize the position is usually filled by a second-year cadet, but I am asking you, Admiral Muti, for permission in this special case."

"Granted, of course, Commander."

Beverly wondered if Claire's jaw was on the floor, too. They both murmured their thanks, and asked if they could have time to think it over.

"Yes. Please think it over—both of you. With your permission, Admiral Muti." The admiral nodded to Wiley. "Cadets? I will see you in class." He was still smiling as he walked out the office door.

Admiral Muti motioned for Beverly and Claire to sit next to her on the window seat overlooking the Golden Gate Bridge. "You are both officially off probation," she said, leaning back in the seat. The sun was just setting along the coast. They watched as the last sunbeams coated the room with yellow and orange—the colors playing across the shimmering Niriad art-harp on the wall. Beverly felt relaxed and tired all at once. For the next hour, the admiral and cadets talked of life, Starfleet—and nothing in particular. It was just good to be there.

CHAPTER

12

"Ouch!"

Beverly jumped back as the porridge popped and bubbled in the pot. She leaned over, turning a dial to adjust the burner on the old stove. The bubbling slowed down and she stirred the mixture. It was her own concoction—remembered from a breakfast her grandmother used to make.

She took a deep breath as the smell of chocolate surrounded her. Claire was taking a chocolate cake out of the oven and setting it to cool on a nearby counter. Mrs. Oner was sitting at a nearby table, chatting with the cadets as they worked.

And after such a busy week, Beverly was glad for the distraction.

"Are you two ever in for a treat," said Beverly, carrying the pot to the kitchen table. Leaning over, she poured out the porridge into three bowls. "This is authentic—well, almost authentic—Scottish porridge with all the trimmings."

"Trimmings?" Claire retorted. She wrinkled her nose as she smelled the porridge in her bowl. "What trimmings?"

"Something my grandmother always used to add to the porridge. Oh, just humor me and taste it," Beverly said, sitting down across from Claire and dipping a spoon into her bowl. She swallowed a spoonful and smiled. "Close . . . real close to the way I remember it."

Claire's eyes went wide as she ate a spoonful of porridge. "Hey, Bev, not bad. Speaking of your grandmother, did you hear from her yet about your adventures at the Academy?"

Beverly smiled at the memory. "Yes. She just smiled and said 'I told you Starfleet Academy was perfect for you—and I noticed you're not so homesick any more.' She knows me."

"Ah, Beverly, she does know you," said Mrs. Oner. "And while we are enjoying your delightful meal, I think Claire has something to tell us," she said, looking at the cadet next to her.

Claire sighed and looked down as she stirred her porridge. "I told Commander Wiley I didn't want to be his assistant."

"Me, too," Beverly added. "I've had enough holodeck adventures for a while. I told him I'd rather concentrate on my medical studies. Plus, I may want to take on some extra courses next semester. But I did suggest that he check out Dewley Breech's record—he would make a great computer assistant."

Claire nodded. "Uh, Beverly, I've made another decision, too."

Beverly held her breath. Claire never called her "Beverly."

"I'm leaving Starfleet Medical," Claire said, looking up at her roommate.

"But—"

"No," she interrupted, holding up a hand. "I've thought long and hard about this. And I've made up my mind."

Beverly's spoon clanged loudly as she dropped it into her bowl. Suddenly, she was not hungry. She knew Claire was still disappointed in her performance during the fated simulation. But with the mystery solved, she thought her roommate was happier. Why would she make such a decision? "Just because of what happened with Max Wiley?" she asked out loud.

"No. It wasn't only that. I feel that Starfleet Medical— or Starfleet in general—is just too competitive for me. There are too many pressures. It just isn't something I want to do anymore."

"But you're one of the best students—" she said, then hesitated. "Oh, no. Are you going to become a professional tennis player?"

Claire laughed. "No, Bev. I'm done swinging a racket. And I don't want you to think I've given up completely," she continued. "I've signed up for a special program. It's for people our age to work and train in medicine specific to a certain planet." She turned and beamed at Mrs. Oner. "And I've been chosen to train on Mrs. Oner's planet, Muldan."

"What?"

"Ah, Beverly," said the Muldanian, turning her smiling face toward Beverly. "You do not know. Here, I am called Mrs. Oner and ambassador. On my planet, I am also called doctor and healer. My empathic and telepathic abilities help me to understand those I cure."

"But Claire doesn't have such abilities," said Beverly.

"That is true, but she will learn about herbs, spices, and remedies to help those who are ailing," answered Mrs. Oner. "She will do well."

Claire laughed. "Mrs. Oner has a great deal of faith in me. But she also showed me the list of plants from Muldan. I know my biggest problem will be to learn how to pronounce all the names."

Beverly didn't share in their laughter. She had no doubt that her roommate would do well on Muldan. But it was the thought of Claire leaving—especially after all they had been through—that hurt the most. More than ever, Beverly was determined to stay in the Academy and become a Starfleet medical doctor. For some reason, she felt Claire would feel the same way.

"Hey, Bev, really, it's all right," Claire said, reaching over and patting Beverly's hand. "I still want to be a doctor, but I've just decided to choose a different path to get there. And I guess my first patient is you. How about a nice cup of lemon tea—not from a replicator?"

Toting a heavy suitcase was never one of Beverly's most favorite pastimes. And now, she was helping Claire carry two bags to Mrs. Oner's in preparation for their flight to Starbase 515 and on to Muldan. She sighed as she read the sign on the front door of the café: Closed. She knew it would be there permanently now.

Several boxes were stacked just inside the door and large metal containers lined one of the walls at the back of the café. The chairs and tables were still there, along with the old stove in the corner of the kitchen. Beverly wondered who would live there—who could take the place of Mrs. Oner.

As Claire went into the kitchen, Beverly walked over to Mrs. Oner in the far corner of the café. She was puzzled as she watched Mrs. Oner carefully wrap several strangely-shaped sculptures in packing, then place them gently in a metal box. The Muldanian woman looked up as Beverly approached. "Ah, these are ancient African sculptures made of okoume wood, Beverly. They are from Admiral Muti. A going-away present, she called them. But I will see her again."

"How do you know?" asked Beverly, tilting her head to the side.

"I know."

"Mrs. Oner," Beverly asked, kneeling down by the older woman as she packed, "what is it like being a doctor?"

Mrs. Oner stopped packing and hesitated. "It is difficult and beautiful," she replied, then resumed packing. "You must help a patient under your care even when they seem to be difficult. You must help a patient even if you do not agree with them." She sealed the lid on the metal box.

"I've certainly learned that lesson in the past week," commented Beverly.

"Then there are problems with overcoming your own attachment to a patient, yet being able to treat them," continued Mrs. Oner. "And there are problems of keep-

115

ing yourself balanced during an emergency—to focus on your patient."

Beverly sighed. "Sometimes I don't think I can do it."

"Ah, Beverly," she said, her eyes twinkling as she looked at the younger woman. "That is the beauty of being a doctor. The challenge of trying to save a life— and to overcome all the obstacles placed in your path."

Beverly leaned over and hugged Mrs. Oner. "I'm really going to miss you. And you know what else?" she asked. "I've almost completely forgotten about being homesick."

A knock on the front door interrupted their conversation. Beverly heard the shuffling of feet on the porch and many voices talking at once.

"Mrs. Oner?" a voice said as the front door opened— and Gren Edut leaned into the room. Right after him, Imto Partigle, Dewley Breech, and T'Kavar pushed their way into the café.

"Ah, welcome, Cadets Gren, Imto, Dewley, and T'Kavar," Mrs. Oner said, standing up and walking toward the cadets. "I am glad you received my message. I did not pack everything yet. I wanted to prepare dinner for all of you, to thank you for helping Beverly and Claire in their quest for the truth. And of course, to celebrate Claire's future as a doctor and healer on Muldan."

She led the cadets to chairs around the largest table in the café. Beverly sat across from Claire. "I can't say I'm glad that you're leaving," she said, "But I really do understand. We have to follow our own way." She smiled at her roommate and held up her cup of tea. "Here's to a doctor's life."

Claire smiled back and raised her cup. "May we always be healers—to others and to ourselves."

Laughter and talk soon filled the room. Beverly looked back into the kitchen. Mrs. Oner took the first plate from a stack on a nearby table, scooped out something from a pot on the stove, and put it on the plate.

"And, Bev," said Claire, watching as the older woman walked over to the table and reached around Beverly from behind, "did I ever tell you that Mrs. Oner makes the best food in this part of the galaxy?"

Beverly's grin widened as she was surrounded by a wonderful smell. In front of her was a perfect plate of Gringle Dash.

About the Author

PATRICIA BARNES-SVARNEY turned in her rock hammer for a word processor many moons ago—and hasn't looked back since. Her nonfiction credits outweigh her fiction credits, and you can often see her name lurking in science magazine articles and along the bindings of books for young readers and adults. As you can tell from this book, she loves to cook; plus, she enjoys reading, rock hunting, astronomy, birding, herb gardening, and hiking. She lives with her husband, countless stuffed animals, and sundry squirrels in Endwell, New York. Her great dream is to someday discover the Theory of Everything—and she hopes it somehow involves chocolate.

About the Illustrator

TODD CAMERON HAMILTON is a self-taught artist who currently lives in Kalamazoo, Michigan. He has been a professional illustrator for the past ten years, specializing in fantasy, science fiction, and horror. Todd is the current president of the Association of Science Fiction and Fantasy Artists. His original works grace many private and corporate collections. He has coauthored two novels and several short stories. When he is not drawing, painting, or writing, his interests include metalsmithing, puppetry, and teaching.